'I thought about you a lot over the weekend.'

Emma swallowed. Her heart tripped. He was bending towards her, his blue eyes capturing hers with an almost magnetic pull. 'I...'

'Thought about me too?' he murmured hopefully.

She had. She couldn't deny it. But would it help either of them if she told him that? Did she need the complication an admission would undoubtedly bring?

Declan leaned closer to her, slowly.

In a second Emma felt her body trembling from the inside out.

'Emma...' he said, his voice low in this last second before his kiss.

Her mouth trembled. She lifted her gaze and stared at him, mesmerised by the yearning she saw in his eyes. The desire to be kissed by him was irresistible, and before she could second-guess the wisdom of it all she was leaning into him.

Declan took her face in his hands, his need materialising in the softest sigh before his mouth found hers. The kiss rolled through his blood, and raw need slammed into him like nothing he had ever known before.

Emma clung to him and the kiss deepened, turned wrenching and wild. She felt a need inside her, an overwhelming need to be touched and held by him.

But it wasn't going to go that far. She felt Declan pulling back, breaking the kiss, slowly, gently.

A long beat of silence while they collected themselves.

'Have we broken every rule in the official partnership handbook?' Declan asked in a deep voice, wrapping her closer.

She licked her lips. 'Possibly...probably.'

Leah Martyn loves to create warm, believable characters for the Mills & Boon® Medical™ Romance series. She is grounded firmly in rural Australia, and the special qualities of the bush are reflected in her stories. For plots and possibilities she bounces ideas off her husband on their early-morning walks. Browsing in bookshops and buying an armful of new releases is high on her list of enjoyable things to do.

Previous titles by the same author:

OUTBACK DOCTOR, ENGLISH BRIDE
THE DOCTOR'S PREGNANCY SECRET
A MOTHER FOR HIS BABY

X

22

Dy
Or

Th
o'

WEDDING IN DARLING DOWNS

BY
LEAH MARTYN

First published in Great Britain 2010
Large Print edition 2011
Harlequin Mills & Boon Limited,
Eton House, 18-24 Paradise Road,
Richmond, Surrey TW9 1SR

© Leah Martyn 2010

ISBN: 978 0 263 21715 5

Harlequin Mills & Boon policy is to use papers that are
natural, renewable and recyclable products and made
from wood grown in sustainable forests. The logging and
manufacturing process conform to the legal environmental
regulations of the country of origin.

Printed and bound in Great Britain
by CPI Antony Rowe, Chippenham, Wiltshire

WEDDING IN DARLING DOWNS

CHAPTER ONE

IT WAS winter. Early morning. And cold.

Emma burrowed her chin more deeply into the roll-collar of her fleece as she jogged the last of the way home across the park.

The cawing of a crow disturbed the peace. Emma slowed her step and looked about her. She loved this time before sun-up. The moist atmosphere never failed to lift her spirits. And heaven knew she could do with a bit of that. Mist was everywhere, as translucent and filmy as a bridal veil. It seemed to have a life of its own, breathing up from the earth, softening the stark winter outlines of the trees.

Emma clicked back into the present, regaining her momentum. She hadn't time to be indulging in fanciful thoughts. Another long day at the surgery loomed. But time for Kingsholme to keep functioning as a viable medical practice was running out. Her father's sudden death almost three months ago had left Emma in disarray. Both personally and professionally. If she didn't line up another partner quickly, the medical practice that had been founded by her grandfather would have to close. One lone doctor, namely *her*, couldn't hope to generate enough income to keep the place functioning.

The end result would be for the practice and the beautiful old home that encompassed it to go under the auctioneer's hammer.

The new owner, perhaps someone with an eye to the tourist potential of the district, would probably turn it into a bed and breakfast. And their little town would be left without a resident medical officer.

Emma's spirits plummeted to a new low. The nerves in her stomach began knotting up again.

I *should* be able to get a doctor interested enough to work here, she berated herself. Even a decent locum who could fill the gap until a suitable partner came along. Perhaps her interviewing technique was all wrong. The few people who had actually showed, had taken one look at the set-up and promptly, if a bit awkwardly, fled.

Lifting the latch on the back gate, she made her way along the path and ran quickly up the steps to the verandah. She had time for a shower and marginally less time for breakfast. And then she'd better open the surgery and start seeing patients.

* * *

In her consulting room later, Emma threw her pen aside and lifted her arms in a long stretch. It had been another crazy morning. She couldn't go on like this. She just couldn't...

A soft tap sounded on her door before it opened. 'Moira—' Emma managed a passable smile for the practice manager '—come to tell me it's lunch time already?'

Moira Connelly, who'd been with the practice for at least twenty years, came into the room and closed the door. She looked pointedly at Emma's untouched cup of tea and the half-eaten muffin and clucked a motherly concern. 'You don't eat enough, Emma.'

Emma lifted a shoulder in a resigned shrug. 'I'll be out in a tick. Perhaps we could open a can of soup for lunch.'

'I'll manage something.' Moira flapped a hand in dismissal. 'Actually, I came to tell you there's a Dr Declan O'Malley here to see you.'

A sudden light leapt into Emma's green eyes. 'Has he come about the job?'

Moira shook her head. 'Apparently, he knew your dad.'

'Oh—' Emma bit her lips together, the grief she felt still raw and unchannelled.

Moira paused, pulling the edges of her cardigan more closely together, as if warding off a sudden chill. 'I expect he wants to offer his condolences.'

'I guess so...' Emma's short ray of hope faded into a heavy sigh. 'Give me a minute, please, Moira and then ask Dr O'Malley to come through.'

Emma watched the door close behind Moira and then swung off her chair and went to stand at the picture window, looking out. She imagined this Dr O'Malley was a contemporary of her father's from Melbourne. In earlier times Andrew Armitage had forged a rather distinguished medical career before the call of *home* had brought him back here to the town of Bendemere on the picturesque Darling Downs in Queensland.

Emma had spent holidays here, been happy here. So it had seemed only natural to come flying home when her world had fallen apart. Her return had coincided with the resignation of her father's practice partner. Emma had stepped in, proud to work alongside her father. In the past year she'd begun to pull the shattered bits of her life together until it was almost making a whole picture again.

Then her father had suffered a massive heart attack, leaving her to cope alone.

Declan O'Malley prowled the reception area. In a few seconds he'd know whether Emma Armitage would welcome his visit or tell him to go to hell.

God, he hoped she'd be reasonable. The situation demanded she be reasonable.

'Oh, Dr O'Malley—' Moira fluttered back into reception. 'Sorry to keep you waiting. Emma was just finishing up.' She waved towards an inner corridor. 'Second door on your left.'

'Thanks.' Declan acknowledged the information with a slight lifting of his hand. He paused outside what was obviously Emma's consulting room, took a deep breath, gave a courtesy knock to warn of his imminent entry, and then moved in with every intention of being at his diplomatic best.

Emma turned from the window. Her throat dried. Every molecule in her body felt as though it had been swiftly rearranged. She'd been expecting a man in her father's age group, a man in his sixties. But Declan O'Malley in no way fitted that description. He looked in the prime of his life, all six feet of him. Mentally roping off the very mixed emotions she felt, she went forward and offered her hand. 'Dr O'Malley.'

'Emma.' Declan ditched formality, enfolding her hand easily within his own. 'Your father told me such a lot about you.'

Well, it's more than he told me about *you*, Emma thought, blinking several times in quick succession, long lashes swooping against her pale cheeks.

'I can imagine what a difficult time this must be for you.' Declan's words filled an uncomfortable gap. 'I would have been in touch before this but I've been out of the country. I've just caught up with things in general.'

She nodded. His voice was deep and resonant. Smooth like red wine. Emma could feel its impact like a thump to her chest, momentarily disarming her. 'Please...have a seat.' She indicated a conversation area in front of the big bay window.

As they settled, Emma took several quick, all-encompassing peeks at him, recording short finger-combed dark hair, a lean face, strong features, olive complexion. And blue eyes reflecting a vivid intensity that could see things she didn't want seen...

Declan looked at the woman he had to deal with here. Emma Armitage was strikingly lovely. She had amazing facial bones and her hair looked cornsilk-soft, blonde and straight, just brushing her shoulders. But it was her eyes that drew him. They were green like the deepest part of the forest, framed within thick tawny lashes. And they were accessing him warily. He had to step carefully here. He didn't want to embarrass her, hurt her. But he'd come on a mission and, somehow, he had to accomplish it.

But how to begin?

'So, how come you knew my father?' In a lightning strike, Emma took the initiative.

Declan refused to be put on the back foot; instead he cut to the chase. 'When I was an intern at St John Bosco's in Melbourne, your father was my boss. I'm where I am today in medicine because of Andrew. In the early days of my training, I was ready to chuck it. Oh, boy was I ready! But your dad talked me out of it. He was an amazing man.'

A new loneliness stabbed through Emma's heart. 'Yes, he was...'

A pause. Awkward. Until Declan resumed gently, 'Over the years I kept in touch with your dad. Any career-change I considered, I ran it past him first. He was my mentor and I considered him my *friend*. And I don't use the word lightly.'

Emma nodded, swallowing past the lump in her throat. 'I appreciate your taking the time to come here.' Her mouth compressed as if shutting off the flow of emotion. 'You must be very busy in your own practice.'

'I'm between jobs, actually. That's another reason why I'm here.'

Emma straightened in her chair, the oddest feeling of unease slithering up her backbone. 'I don't understand.'

Declan's perceptions whipped into high awareness. Something in her eyes and the defensive little tilt of her chin held him back from explaining further. The last thing he needed was for her to start resenting him before they could speak properly. So, softly-softly. 'Uh...this could take a while.' He glanced briefly at his watch. 'Could we perhaps have a spot of lunch somewhere and talk?'

Emma held back a harsh laugh. He just had no idea. 'I don't have time to go out to lunch, Dr O'Malley. Patients will be arriving soon for the afternoon surgery.'

'You're the sole practitioner?'

'Yes,' she said, thinking that was another story in itself.

He'd assumed she'd have engaged a locum, but obviously not. Declan thought quickly. Emma Armitage had a brittleness about her—she was obviously worked to death. He cursed his lack of foresight and sought to remedy it swiftly. 'Understood.' He gave a brief shrug. 'I'm here and available. Put *me* to work.'

So, what was he saying? That he'd share her patient list? Emma's eyes widened. She didn't want to be blunt but she had only this man's word he was a competent doctor. First and foremost, she had a duty of care to her patients... She turned her head slightly, raising a hand to sweep her loose fair hair away from her neck. 'Is that a good idea, do you think?'

Declan sat riveted. Her little restive movement had briefly exposed her nape, with skin as tender and sweet as a baby's. He tried without success to dismiss the unexpected zip of awareness through his gut. What was the question again? Idiot. Got it. 'Sorry.' He gave an apologetic twist of his hand. 'You'll need some ID.' Reaching back, he took out his wallet and spun it open in front of her. 'Driver's licence.'

Emma nodded, registering that the photo on the licence matched the face of the man sitting opposite her. So he was who he claimed he was.

'My card as well.' He held out the buff-coloured business card towards her.

Frowning a bit, Emma took it, almost dazzled by the impressive array of letters after his name. 'You completed your orthopaedic speciality in Edinburgh, Scotland?'

His hesitation was palpable. Then he said, 'Yes. It was always the discipline I felt drawn to.'

She handed the licence back with the ghost of a smile but retained his card. 'Should I be addressing you as Professor O'Malley, then?'

'I wouldn't think so.' In a second his eyes were filled with unfathomable depth and shadows. 'Declan will do just fine. So—' he slid his wallet back into his pocket '—going to let me loose on your patients, then?'

'Why wouldn't I?' Emma felt a curious lightening of her spirits. To be able to share her workload, even for a few hours, would be wonderful. 'I'll give you the ones who like a good chat.'

'I guess I asked for that.' Declan's look was rueful and he uncurled to his feet. 'I'll grab a burger somewhere and my bag and be back in—' he checked his watch '—twenty minutes?'

Swept along by his enthusiasm, Emma stood hastily. 'Take whatever time you need.' She began to usher him out. 'You can use Dad's consulting room.'

Declan stopped, looked down at her, his expression closed. 'If you're sure?'

Emma nodded, leading him down the corridor to the room next to her own. She opened the door and went in.

Declan followed hesitantly. Soft early afternoon light streamed in through the windows, leaving a dappled pattern across the large desk and the big leather chair behind it. A big chair for a big man, Declan thought. A man with a big heart that had in the end let him down far earlier than it should have.

'It's been cleaned but basically everything is as Dad left it.' Emma moved across to touch the tips of her fingers to the rosewood patina of the desktop.

Declan felt emotion drench him. Yet he knew what he felt at the man's loss was only a fraction of what his daughter must be feeling. He spun to face her, questioning softly, 'Are you sure about this, Emma?'

'Quite sure. It will be good to see the place being used again.' The words were husky, as though she was pushing them through a very tight throat.

Declan wanted to reach out to her. Hold her close. Feel the press of her body against his. Take her grief into himself... Oh, for crying out loud! He cleared his throat. 'I'll see you back here, then, in a half-hour or so.'

'Feel free to come straight through and get yourself set up,' Emma said as they left the consulting room and she pulled the door closed. 'I'll just need to make a call and verify your registration before you take surgery.'

Declan inclined his head, acknowledging her eyes were clearly weighing the effect of her statement on him. He gave a mental shrug. As far as his accreditation went, he had nothing to hide. 'Good,' he agreed. 'You should do that.'

'And I'll brief Moira,' Emma added. 'She'll make sure the patients find you.'

'Moira.' Declan lifted a dark brow. 'The lady I spoke to in reception, right?'

Emma nodded. 'She's been with us for years. I sometimes think she could treat most of the patients herself.' Her eyes lit impishly, her full mouth hooking into a half smile.

The impact of that curve of her lips hit him like a sandbag to the solar-plexus. He flicked back the edges of his jacket, jamming his hands low on his hips. 'Let's try to push through early, then.' He paused, his blue gaze roaming over her in an almost physical caress. 'We do need to talk, Emma.'

For a second Emma felt as though she could hardly breathe, his proximity sending a warm rush of want to every part of her body. Feminine places she'd almost forgotten existed. She pulled back, regaining her space. 'We'll arrange something...'

Even though the circumstances weren't ideal, it was good to be back in a consulting room with his feet under a desk again, Declan thought. At least he was doing something useful and if it lasted no more than the rest of the day, he'd give it his best shot.

He was amazed how the time flew. He saw a steady stream of patients, each without exception with a comment about his presence in the practice. He'd answered as honestly as he could, 'I'm helping out Dr Armitage for the moment.' And whether that situation became permanent still depended on so many things. So many.

He called in his final patient for the day, Carolyn Jones. She looked anxiously at Declan. 'I was expecting to see Emma—Dr Armitage.'

'Emma's passed some of her patients over to me today, Mrs Jones,' Declan offloaded with a cheerful smile. 'I'll do my best to help.'

Carolyn gripped her handbag more tightly. 'I... really just wanted a chat...'

'That's fine,' Declan encouraged, leaning back in his chair, his look expectant. 'I'm here to listen.'

'I want to go back on my sleeping pills. I've tried to do without them for a couple of months now but I just can't manage—' Carolyn stopped and swallowed heavily.

For a second Declan considered a quick consult with Emma. But she had enough on her plate. He could handle this. He leaned forward, speed-reading the patient notes.

The lady was sixty-one but there was nothing leaping out at him to warrant extra caution. He raised his gaze, asking, 'Is there a reason why you can't sleep, Carolyn?'

'I've a difficult family life. Emma knows about it—'

'I see. Suppose you tell me about it as well and see how we go?'

Carolyn lifted her shoulders in a long sigh. 'My husband, Nev, and I are bringing up our three grandchildren. Their ages range from seven to ten.'

'Hard going, then,' Declan surmised gently. 'What circumstances caused this to come about?'

Carolyn gave a weary shrug. 'The whole town knows about it. Our son was a soldier serving overseas. He was killed by a roadside mine. Our daughter-in-law, Tracey, took off and then got in with the wrong crowd. Started seeing someone else. She was always a bit *flighty.*'

Declan raised his eyebrows at the old-fashioned word.

'She's with this new boyfriend now. We've heard they're into drugs. I don't understand how she could just dump her children...'

Declan's caring instincts went out to his patient. But, on the other hand, there were strategies she could try that might induce natural sleep—

'The children are still unsettled, especially at night,' Carolyn said, interrupting his train of thought. 'I just can't get off to sleep and then I'm useless the next day.' She paused and blinked. 'I've really had enough....'

So, crisis time then. Declan thought quickly. As a general rule, sleeping pills were prescribed in small doses and only for a limited time-span. But his patient sounded desperate—desperate enough to... He got to his feet. 'Carolyn, excuse me a moment. I've been out of the country for a while. I'll just need to recheck on dosage and so on.'

Declan came out of his office the same time as Emma emerged from hers. Her brows flicked in question. 'Finished for the day?'

'Not quite.' He accompanied her along to reception. 'Actually, I wanted a word about a patient, Carolyn Jones.'

'The family have ongoing problems,' Emma said quietly.

'I gathered that.' Declan backed himself against the counter and folded his arms. 'Carolyn wants to go back on her sleeping pills. I wondered about her stability.'

'You're asking me whether she's liable to over-dose on them?'

'Just double-checking.'

'She cares too much about those children to do anything silly,' Emma said.

'Quite. But still—'

'The sleepers Carolyn takes are quite mild,'

Emma cut in. 'They don't produce a hangover effect next day.'

A beat of silence until Declan broke it. 'You realize more than two weeks on those things and she's hooked?'

Oh, for heaven's sake! Emma almost ground her teeth. Declan O'Malley needed to stand outside the rarefied air of his theatre suite and realize family practice was about people not protocol. 'If you're so concerned, make it a stopgap solution. In the meantime, I'll try to figure out some other way to help her. But if Carolyn can't get sleep, she'll go dotty. Then where will the family be?' she pointed out.

'OK...' Declan raised a two-fingered salute in a peace sign. This obviously wasn't the time to start a heated discussion with the lady doctor. 'I'll go ahead and write her script.' He took a couple of steps forward and then wheeled back. 'Are you around for a while?'

Emma felt the nerves in her stomach tighten. What was on his mind now? 'My last patient just left so I'll be here.'

'Good.' Declan's eyes glinted briefly. 'I'm sorry to push it, but we do need to talk.'

Emma twitched her shoulders into a barely per-ceptible shrug and watched him go back to his consulting room. Then she went into the work space behind reception and began slotting files back into place.

Moira joined her. With the information Emma had discreetly passed on to her about the new doctor, Moira's eyes were rife with speculation. 'Do you think he'll stay?'

At the thought, Emma managed a dry smile. 'I haven't offered him a job yet. And, even if I did, I expect Dr O'Malley has far more exciting challenges than working in a run-down practice in a country town.'

'You never know.' Moira's voice held a bracing optimism.

No, you never did. Thinking of her father's untimely death, Emma could only silently agree. 'Moira, it's way past your home time. I'll lock up.'

'If you're sure?' Moira looked uncertain.

'I'll be fine. Go.' Emma flapped a hand. 'And have a nice evening.'

There was still no sign of Declan some ten minutes later. Carolyn was obviously still with him. Perhaps it would help her to talk to a different practitioner, Emma thought philosophically. Heaven knew, she herself had no extra time to allot to her needy patients. Well, even if Declan helped only *one* of her patients in the short time he was here, it was a plus. Deciding there was no use hanging round in reception, she went through to the staffroom.

Declan found her there. He gave a rat-a-tat on the door with the back of his hand to alert her.

Emma's head came up, her eyes blinking against his sudden appearance. 'Hi...'

'Hi, yourself.' One side of his mouth inched upward and a crease formed in his cheek as he smiled. 'I smelled coffee.'

Emma averted her gaze to blot out the all-male physical imprint.

In a couple of long strides, he'd crossed the room to her.

Emma lifted the percolator, her fingers as unsteady as her heartbeat. 'Milk and sugar's there on the tray.'

'Thanks.' He took the coffee, added a dollop of milk and lifted the cup to his mouth. 'Could we sit for a minute?'

Emma indicated the old kitchen table that been in the staff room for as long as she could remember. 'You were a long time with Carolyn. Everything OK?' she asked as they took their places on opposite sides of the table.

'I hope so.' Declan's long fingers spanned his coffee mug and he said thoughtfully, 'We talked a bit and I suggested a few things. Some tai chi, a good solid walk in the early evening could help her relax enough to induce a natural sleep. Even a leisurely swim would be beneficial.'

'The school has a pool but it's not open to the public.'

'Pity. She's obviously quite tense.'

'And it's a situation that's happening more and more,' Emma agreed. 'Grandparents taking on the caring role for their grandchildren. Even here in this small community, there are families in similar circumstances as the Joneses.'

Declan took a long mouthful of his coffee. 'Does Bendemere have anything like a support group for them? Somewhere they can air their fears and worries in a safe environment?'

Emma resisted the urge to shriek. 'This isn't the city, Dr O'Malley. We're a bit short of facilitators and psychologists who could lead a group.'

'But a doctor could.'

Was he serious? 'Don't you think I would if I could?' she flashed. 'I'm so stretched now, I—'

'No, Emma, you're misunderstanding me.' His look was guarded and cool. 'I meant *me*—I could help.'

'You?' Emma huffed her disbelief. She wasn't understanding any of this. 'Are you saying you want to stay on here?'

'You need a practice partner, don't you?'

'But you know nothing about the place!' Emma's

thoughts were spinning. 'Nothing about the viability of the practice. Nothing about *me*.'

He stared at her for a long moment. 'I know you're Andrew's daughter.'

'And you'd make a life-changing decision on the basis of that?' Emma's voice had a husky edge of disquiet.

Oh, hell. He was doing this all wrong. No wonder she was confused. He'd meant to lead up to things gently and objectively, explain himself, choose his words carefully. But just getting his head around Emma's crippling workload, the plight of Carolyn Jones and others like her had spurred him on to get matters sorted and quickly.

'Emma—' He paused significantly. 'I didn't just come here to offer my condolences. There's another reason why I'm here in Bendemere.'

Emma tried to grasp the significance of his words. 'Perhaps you'd better explain.'

Declan watched as she drew herself up stiffly, almost as if she were gathering invisible armour around her. He knew what he was about to tell her would come as a shock, maybe even wound her deeply. But he had to do it. 'Your father contacted me shortly before his death. He offered to sell me his share of the practice. I'm here to arrange payment and finalise the details of our partnership.'

Emma's mouth fell open and then snapped shut.

She clutched the edge of the table for support, becoming aware of her heart thrashing to a sickening rhythm inside her chest. 'I don't believe Dad would have done something like that.'

'I have a letter of confirmation from your father and the legal documents.'

'Dad wouldn't have just *thrust* someone on me. Someone I didn't even know!' She felt the pitch of her anger and emotion rising and didn't care. 'And I don't have to accept your money, Dr O'Malley, nor do I *have* to take you on as my practice partner.'

Declan's gaze narrowed on her flushed face, the angry tilt of her small chin. Damn! He hadn't reckoned on any of this. 'It was what your father wanted, Emma.'

Emma gave a hard little laugh. 'Emotional blackmail will get you absolutely nowhere, Dr O'Malley.'

'Please!' With a reflex action Declan's head shot up, his vivid blue gaze striking an arc across the space between them. 'Give me a little credit. I realize this has come as a shock to you. And I'm sorry. I'd hoped Andrew might have given you some idea of what he wanted, paved the way a bit, but obviously time ran out on him. But we can't leave things here, Emma. We really can't.' His mouth compressed briefly. 'I suggest we take a break and let things settle a bit. I'm staying at the Heritage Hotel. We could link up there later this evening and talk further. Dinner around seven. Does that suit you?'

'Fine,' Emma responded bluntly. It seemed she had no choice in the matter.

'Let's meet at the bar, then.' Declan grabbed at the grudging acceptance.

CHAPTER TWO

EMMA hitched up her little shoulder bag and determinedly pushed open the heavy plate glass door
of the restaurant. She loved this place. As it was
winter, the lovely old fireplace was lit, sending
out warmth and flickering patterns to the wood-
panelled walls. The atmosphere was charming and
tonight was the first time she'd come here since…
Her teeth caught on her lower lip. She and Dad
had come here often. The Sunday lunch at the
Heritage was legendary.

But this evening her dinner companion was
someone far different than her father.

Heart thrumming, Emma made her way along
the parquet flooring towards the bar. Declan was
there already. She saw him at once, his distinctive
dark head turning automatically, almost as if he'd
sensed her approach. A shower of tingles began
at the base of her backbone, spiralling upwards
and engulfing her. She swallowed. He was wearing dark jeans and an oatmeal-coloured sweater
that looked soft and cuddly. Oh, get real, Emma!

Cuddles and Declan O'Malley were about as compatible as oil and water.

'Hello again.' Declan nodded almost formally. And blinked. Wow! Gone was the harassed-looking medico. Emma Armitage could have sauntered in from the catwalk. She was wearing black leggings and a long-sleeved, long-line silver-grey T-shirt, a huge silky scarf in a swirl of multicolour around her throat. And knee-high boots. 'You look amazing.'

'Thanks.' Her shrug was so slight he hardly saw it. 'I love your outfit too.'

So, the lady did have a sense of humour after all. A quirky one at that. Declan's grin unfolded lazily, his eyes crinkling at the corners. 'We seem to have that sorted, so let's try to enjoy our evening, shall we? Would you like something to drink?'

In a leggy, graceful movement, Emma hitched herself up on to one of the high bar stools. 'A glass of the house red would be nice, thanks.'

For a while they talked generalities and then Declan glanced at his watch. 'I reserved us a table. Shall we go through?'

'It's rather crowded for a week night,' Emma said stiltedly as they took their places in the restaurant adjoining the bar.

'I've been quite taken with the town,' Declan rejoined. 'Tell me a bit about its history.'

Emma did her best to comply and it wasn't until they'd come to the end of their meal and were sitting over coffee she said pointedly, 'It's been a long day, could we wind things up so we can both get on about our business?'

'OK, then.' Declan's moody blue eyes were fixed unflinchingly on hers. 'I'll get straight to the point. About six months ago I received a letter from your father telling me about his deterioration in health.'

For a few seconds Emma stared at him in numb disbelief. 'Dad told *you* and he didn't tell me? Why? I was his daughter, for heaven's sake.'

Declan could hardly bear to watch her grief. 'I know it sounds an old chestnut, Emma,' he said gently, 'but perhaps he didn't want to upset you any further than you had been. You had other things going on in your life, didn't you?'

Emma's face was tightly controlled. 'What did Dad tell you about that?'

'Almost nothing—just that you'd had a few personal problems.'

Like mopping up the emotional fallout after her rat of a fiancé had dumped her for her best friend...

'And that you'd come back to work in the practice,' Declan finished diplomatically.

Emma curled her hands into a tight knot on her

lap. 'What did he tell you about his health? That he had only a short time to live?'

Declan's frown deepened. 'Nothing like that. But, from what he told me, I drew my own conclusions. If it hadn't been for the fact that I, myself, was in somewhat of a personal crisis at the time, I'd have come back to Australia to see Andrew immediately. Instead, I called him. He was concerned for you, for the future of the practice if the worst happened. We talked at length. It was then he offered to sell me his half of the practice.'

'I see.' Emma swallowed through a suddenly dry throat. But she understood now why her father hadn't told her anything about his plans. He would have had to reveal the uncertain state of his health. So instead he'd trusted Declan O'Malley to set things right. But did that mean she had to accept him as her partner? She didn't think so. 'I'm sure Dad wouldn't have wanted you interfering in my life.'

'That's not what Andrew had in mind, Emma.'

'So, you're here as some kind of…white knight?' she grated bitterly.

'I'm here because I want to be here,' Declan said simply. 'Because it seems like a worthwhile thing to do. You need a partner. I need a job. Isn't that the truth of it?'

She looked at him warily. 'Why do you need a

job? You obviously have medical qualifications beyond the norm. Career-wise, the world should be your playground. Why aren't you working in your chosen discipline somewhere?'

'It's a long story.'

'There's plenty of coffee in the pot,' Emma countered. 'And we're quite private here.'

Declan felt the familiar grind in his guts at the thought of rehashing everything.

At his continued silence, something like resentment stirred in Emma and she couldn't let go of it. 'Dr O'Malley, if you've ideas of entering into partnership with me, then I need to know what I'm getting. That's only fair, isn't it?'

He took a long breath and let it go. 'My surgical career is, to all intents and purposes, finished. I can't operate any longer.'

Faint shock widened Emma's eyes. How awful. She knew only too well what it was like to have your world collapse with no redress possible. 'I'm sorry.'

'Thank you.' The words escaped mechanically from his lips.

And that was it? Emma took in the sudden tight set of his neck and shoulders. He had to know she needed more information. Much more than the bald statement he'd offered. She felt about for the right words to help him. But in the end it was a simple, softly spoken, 'What happened?'

Declan rubbed a hand across his forehead. 'After I'd completed my general surgery training, I decided to go ahead and specialize in orthopaedics.' His blue eyes shone for a moment. 'On a good day when everything in the OR goes right and you know it's your skill that's enabling a patient to regain their mobility, their normal life, and in some instances their whole livelihood…it's empowering and humbling all rolled into one.'

'Yes, I imagine it is,' Emma said, but she had the feeling he had hardly heard.

'I was fortunate enough to be accepted at St Mary's in Edinburgh.'

Emma's eyes widened. 'Their training programme is legendary. I believe they take only the brightest and best.'

'I was lucky,' he said modestly.

Hardly. Obviously, he was seriously gifted. Which fact made Declan O'Malley's reasons for opting to come in as her partner in a country practice odd indeed, she thought, noticing he'd hadn't touched his coffee. Instead, he'd spanned his fingers around the cup, holding on to it like some kind of lifeline.

'After a long stint in Scotland, I'd decided to head back home. I was still finalizing dates when I had a call from an Aussie mate. He was coming over for a holiday in the UK, beginning in Scotland. I postponed my plans and Jack and I bought a couple of motorbikes.'

'Fuel-wise cheaper than cars, I guess,' was Emma's only comment.

'Jack and I found a couple of high-powered beauties for sale locally. Those bikes took us everywhere. Life was sweet—until we had the accident.'

Emma winced and she automatically put her hand to her heart. 'How?'

He gave a grim smile. 'A foggy afternoon, an unfamiliar road. A bit too much speed. And a truck that came out of nowhere. Jack received a broken leg. I was somewhat more compromised. I ended up with lumbar injuries.' He expanded on the statement with technical language, ending with, 'The outcome was partial paralysis in my left leg.' He grimaced as if the memory was still fresh.

Emma gripped her hands tightly. He must have been sick with worry and conjecture. And fear. Her antagonism faded and her heart went out to him. 'What was the result? I mean, you don't appear to have any deficit in your movement.'

His eyes took on a dull bleakness. 'I've regained most of it but my muscles are unpredictable, my toes still get numb from time to time. Added to that, I can't stand for excessively long periods. And that's what orthopaedic surgeons have to do. You need to have muscle strength, be in control. I can't risk a patient's life by breaking down in the middle of a long operation. So, career-wise, I'm stuffed.'

'But you could do other kinds of surgery,' Emma said hopefully.

'I don't even want to think about that. I want to do what I was trained to do—what I do—*did* best.'

But sometimes you had to compromise. Emma knew that better than most. 'You could lecture, Declan.'

He made a disgusted sound. 'Take up a *chair* in a hallowed hall somewhere? That's not me. I'm a doer. I'd rather change direction entirely.'

'In other words, come in as my partner—' She broke off. 'You might hate it.'

'I don't think so.' Blue eyes challenged her although his mouth moved in the ghost of a wry smile. When she remained silent, he went on, 'Emma, don't you think it's just possible Andrew considered he was acting in the best interests of *both* of us? He knew the extent of my injuries, the uncertain state of my career in medicine and he knew, without him, you were going to need a partner—someone you could trust. And you *can* trust me, Emma,' he assured her sincerely.

Emma felt almost sick with vulnerability. Heaven knew there was no one else beating the door down to come and work with her. But this man? On the other hand, what choice did she have? He had all the power on his side and, she suspected, the determination that her father's wishes would be carried out. There was really no get-out clause here. None at all. 'How do we go about setting things in motion, then?' Her voice was small and formal.

Declan breathed the greatest sigh of relief. They'd got to the trickiest hurdle and jumped it. 'You're overworked and under-capitalised. If we tackle the problems together, Kingsholme could be brought up to its potential again. Why don't we give it six months? If we find we can't work together, I'll get out.'

'And where will that leave me?'

'Hopefully, with a fully functioning practice. You'd have no difficulty attracting a new partner and I'd recoup my investment. It would be a win-win situation for both of us.'

Emma knew the decision had already been made for her. She wanted to—*needed* to—keep Kingsholme. Declan O'Malley had been Dad's choice of a suitable practice partner for her. She had to trust his judgement and go along with that. Otherwise, she was back to the mind-numbing uncertainty of the past weeks. 'Have you come prepared to stay, then?'

'I've brought enough gear to keep me going for a while.' Declan kept his tone deliberately brisk. 'If it suits you, I'll continue at the surgery until Friday and then, on the weekend, we can go over what practical changes need to be made. I'd imagine you'd have a few ideas of your own about that?'

'It depends on how much money you want to spend,' Emma shot back with the faintest hint of cynicism.

He answered levelly, 'There'll be enough.'

On Friday afternoon, they held a quick consult after surgery. 'What time do you want to begin tomorrow?' Emma asked.

Declan lifted his medical case up on the counter. 'I'm flexible. What suits you?'

'I need to do an early hospital round. We could meet after that.'

'Why can't I come to the hospital with you?'

Emma looked uncertain. 'It's all pretty basic medicine we do here.'

'And nothing I'd be interested in?' Declan's gaze clouded. 'Emma, if we're partners, we share duties. Right?'

She coloured slightly. 'I was just pointing out there'll be none of the drama associated with Theatres.'

'So, it'll be a change of pace. I can handle that.'

Could he, though? Emma wished she felt more certain. On the other hand, why not think positively? She'd already capitulated over him becoming her partner. It was time to just get on with things. 'Hospital at eight o'clock, then? I'll give you the tour.'

'That's what I want to hear,' he drawled with his slow smile.

For a split second Emma registered a zinging awareness between them. Raw and immediate. Like the white-heat of an electric current. She repressed a gasp. Declan O'Malley exuded sex appeal in spades. He was about to step in as her practice partner. And they were going to be working very closely together for at least the next six months...

Emma had enjoyed her Saturday morning run. Leaning forward, hands on the verandah railings, she breathed deeply and began to warm down.

'Great morning for it,' a male voice rumbled behind her and she jumped and spun round, her heart skittering.

Emma straightened, one hand clenched on the railings, her senses on high alert, as Declan O'Malley came up the steps. His sudden appearance had made her flustered and unsure. 'I run most mornings.' She felt his eyes track over her and, before she could move or comprehend, he'd lifted a hand and knuckled her cheek ever so gently. Emma felt her breath jam.

'It's good to see those shadows gone,' he said, his voice throaty and low and further tugging on her senses. His eyes beckoned hers until she lifted her gaze. 'I gather you slept well?'

She nodded, breath rushing into the vacuum of her lungs. She'd slept well for the first time in weeks. She wasn't about to analyse the reason. But she had a fair idea it was all to do with the fact that at least for the next little while, her future was settled. Her teeth caught on her lower lip. 'I thought we were to meet at the hospital.'

Hands rammed in his back pockets, Declan shifted his stance slightly as if to relieve tense muscles. 'I was awake early. Thought I might come over and persuade you to have breakfast with me.'

'Or you could stay here and have breakfast with *me*,' Emma rushed out. 'I'm sure I could cobble something together.'

'I didn't mean to gatecrash—'

'You're not.' She took a thin breath. 'Give me a minute to have a shower and change.'

He followed her inside to the kitchen. 'I could knock us up some breakfast—that's if you don't mind someone else rattling around in your kitchen?'

'Not remotely.' In a reflex action, Emma jerked the zipper closed on her track top right up to her chin. 'Uh...I did a shop last night. There's plenty of stuff in the fridge.' She almost ran from the room.

Sheesh! Declan spun away, thumping the heel of his hand to his forehead. Why on earth had he done that? *Touched* her. He hadn't meant it to happen but at that moment his hand had seemed to have a life of its own. Oh, good grief. Surely, the idea had been to reassure her he was trustworthy. Well, that premise was shot. Instead, he'd gone to the other extreme and created a damn great elephant in the room. He hissed out a breath of frustration and tried to take stock of the kitchen. He'd promised her breakfast. He'd better start delivering.

Emma showered in record time, towelled dry and dressed quickly in comfortable cargos and a ruby-red sweater. She wasn't about to drive herself crazy thinking about earlier. It was hardly a professional thing for Declan to have done. What she couldn't work out was her instinctive response to his touch... Oh, Lord. Suddenly, her body was stiff with tension. Almost jerkily, she lifted her hands, bunching her hair from her shoulders and letting it spiral away. At least he'd got on with the breakfast. There was a gorgeous smell of grilling bacon coming from the kitchen.

'How's it going?' Emma asked, buzzing back into the kitchen, determined not to start walking on eggshells around him. They were about to become partners in practice. Nothing else. 'Find everything?'

Declan looked up from the stove. 'No worries. It's a great kitchen.'

'Tottering with age but very user-friendly,' Emma agreed. Opening the door of the fridge, she peered in and located the orange juice. She poured two glasses and handed one across to Declan.

'Thanks. I'm doing bacon and scrambled eggs.'

'Lovely.'

Declan lifted his glass and drained it slowly as he watched the eggs begin to thicken and fluff. He could get used to this. The warmth and the clutter of the old-fashioned kitchen. The comforting aroma of food cooking. The feeling of solidness, of family. The place just breathed it. He could get some idea now of how desperate Emma had been to hang on to her home. 'Your idea?' He pointed to the sun-catcher crystal that dangled from the window in front of the sink.

Her tiny smile blossomed to a grin. 'My *alternative* period. You about done here?'

'I hope it's up to scratch,' he said, catching the drift of her flowery shampoo as her head topped his shoulder.

'Mmm, smells good.' Emma gave him a quick nod of approval. 'I'll get the plates.'

'I used to run a bit,' Declan said as they settled over breakfast.

'You can't now?'

His mouth pulled down. 'I seem to be stuck with a set of prescribed exercises these days.'

Emma looked up sharply with a frown. Did that mean he didn't trust his legs on a simple run? 'I understood you to say it was standing for long periods you had trouble with. Short bursts of running would seem OK, surely? And drawing all that fresh air into your bloodstream works magic.'

Well, he knew that. 'Maybe it'll happen. In time.'

So, end of discussion. Emma pursed her mouth into a thoughtful moue, realizing suddenly that her own emotional baggage didn't seem nearly as weighty as her soon-to-be-partner's. Determinedly, she pulled out her social skills and managed to create enough general conversation to get them through the rest of the meal. She glanced at her watch, surprised to see the time had gone so quickly. She swung up from the table. 'If you'll start clearing away, I'll just feed the cat.'

Declan gave a rusty chuckle, looking sideways to where the big tabby sprawled indolently on the old-fashioned cane settee. 'Looks like he wants room service.'

Emma snorted. 'Lazy creature. I think the mice run rings around him. He belonged to Mum.'

Declan hesitated with a response, a query in his eyes.

'She moved back to Melbourne about a year ago,' Emma enlightened him thinly. 'Dad bought her an art gallery in St Kilda. It had an apartment attached so the whole set-up suited her perfectly and Dad went there as often as he could before he died. She never really felt at home here in rural Queensland. Missed the buzz of the city, her friends.'

Declan was thoughtful as he stood to his feet, processing the information. At least now he knew where the bulk of Andrew's estate had gone and why the practice was all but running on goodwill. And why Emma's stress levels must have been immense as a result.

Between them, they put the kitchen to rights in a few minutes. Hanging the tea towel up to dry, Emma felt an odd lightness in her spirits.

'Emma, I wonder if you could spare a few minutes now? There are a couple of business decisions I'd like to run past you.'

His voice had a firm edge to it and Emma came back to earth with a thud. 'Let's go through to Dad's—*your* surgery,' she substituted shortly. 'I'll give the hospital a call and let them know we'll be along a bit later than planned.'

They took their places at the big rosewood desk. 'Fire away,' Emma invited, locking her arms around her middle as if to protect herself.

Declan moved his position, sitting sideways in his chair, his legs outstretched and crossed at the ankles. 'First up, I'll need to see some figures from your accountant. Could you arrange that, please?'

'I do have some current figures,' she replied. 'I organized that when I needed to see what state the practice was in after Dad—' She stopped. 'I'll get them for you directly. Perhaps you'd like to study them over the weekend.'

'Thanks.' He nodded almost formally. 'That will help a lot. Now, your office system—'

'Yes?'

'It seems a bit outdated. You obviously have

computers installed but no one seems to be using them.'

She'd wondered when they'd get to that. 'I encouraged Dad to get them soon after I moved back and we had the appropriate software installed. Moira did an evening course at the local high school, but at the end of it she said it was all beyond her. Dad said he felt more comfortable with his own way of doing things.'

'I see.'

'I tried to get things operational myself, but then, with Dad gone, it all came to a screeching halt. Any time I had to spare has had to go on face-to-face consults.'

'The system must be got up and running,' he insisted. 'If it's too onerous for Moira, then she'd be better—'

'I won't let you sack her, Declan,' Emma swiftly interjected.

He raised his head and looked at her coolly. 'Emma, don't go second-guessing me, please. I was about to add, Moira would be better staying with what she does best. She's obviously invaluable to the practice. She knows the patients well and that helps facilitate appointments. But what we do need is someone with expertise who can come in on a permanent basis and get our patient lists up to date and their medical history on to the computers. Can you think of anyone suitable?'

'Not offhand,' she said stiffly. It all made sense though and, belatedly, she realized the shortcomings he'd pointed out had probably been one of the reasons the doctors she'd interviewed had vetoed working here. 'I'll have a chat to Moira. Better still, I'll call her now.' She felt almost goaded into action, reaching for the phone on his desk. She hit Moira's logged-in home number and, after a brief conversation, replaced the receiver in its cradle. Raising her gaze, she looked directly at Declan. 'Moira's coming in now. She says she may have a few ideas. I hope that's in order?'

Declan spread his hands in compliance. He wished Emma didn't see him as the bad guy here. But he'd promised Andrew he'd do what he could to save the practice and if along the way he had to tread on a few toes—gently, of course–then he'd do it. He hauled his legs up and swivelled them under the desk. 'I noticed we don't seem to have the services of a practice nurse. What's the situation there?'

'We used to have one, Libby Macklin. She took maternity leave, intending to come back, but found it was just too much with the demands of the baby. We didn't get round to replacing her.'

Declan placed his hands palms down on the desk. 'Would she like to come back, do you think?'

Emma nodded. 'I see her quite often. The baby's older now, of course, and Libby's managing much better. I know she'd appreciate some work but I just haven't been in a position to offer her any...'

'Sound her out then,' Declan said, refusing to acknowledge Emma's wistful expression.

'I'll go and see her after we've been to the hospital. Now, about patient lists.'

'I'm listening.'

'I'm not sure how you'd like to work it, but perhaps we could do a clean swap? You'd take over Dad's patients,' she suggested.

'That sounds fair. And I'm thinking we could schedule a weekly practice meeting, air anything problematic then. Suit you?'

Heck, did she even have a choice in the matter? A resigned kind of smile dusted Emma's lips. 'Fine.'

Declan frowned and glanced at his watch. 'How long will Moira be?'

'Not long. She lives only a few minutes away.'

'Yoo-hoo, it's me!' As if on cue, Moira's quick tap along the corridor accompanied her greeting.

Declan uncurled to his feet and dragged up another chair. 'Thanks for doing this, Moira.'

'No worries.' She flapped a hand and leant

forward confidentially. 'I'll get straight to the point. My granddaughter is looking for work.'

'Jodi?' Emma's gaze widened in query. 'I thought she was full-time at McGinty's stables.'

Moira's mouth turned down. 'James, the youngest son, has returned home so he's taken over much of the track work. Jodi's there only one day a week now.'

Declan exchanged a quick guarded look with Emma. Moira was obviously a doting grandmother but they couldn't afford to be giving jobs away on her say-so. 'Moira, we'd need to have a chat to Jodi about what the job here entails,' he stressed diplomatically.

'Of course you would.' Moira smiled. 'That's why I've brought her in with me. She's outside in reception.'

'Ask her to come in then,' Declan said briefly, turning to Emma as Moira left the room. 'What do you think?' he asked quietly. 'You obviously know this young woman. Are we doing the right thing here?'

'Jodi is very bright. Providing her technical skills are up to speed, then I think she'll do a good job. Oh—here she is now.'

Declan got to his feet again as Jodi bounded in, all youthful spirits and sparkling eyes. 'Hi.' She linked the two doctors with a wide white smile.

'Jodi.' Declan stuck out his hand in greeting. 'Declan O'Malley. Emma you know, of course.'

'Hello, Jodi.' Emma beckoned the teenager to a seat. 'Moira says you're looking for some work.'

'Yes, I am.' Jodi slid her huge leather satchel from her shoulder and on to the floor beside her chair. 'Nan's told me a bit about what you need here. I could easily manage to give you three days a week, if that suits. I work track at McGinty's on Fridays and I've just got a day's work at the supermarket on Thursdays. So I could give you from Monday to Wednesday.'

Declan leaned back in his chair and folded his arms. 'How old are you, Jodi?'

'Eighteen. At present I'm taking a gap year before I start Uni.'

'What are you studying?' Declan asked.

'Applied science. Eventually, I want to be associated with the equine industry, combine research and field work. Horses and their welfare are my great passion. I'll need to do my doctorate, of course.'

'That's really worthwhile, Jodi,' Emma said warmly. 'Best of luck with your studies.'

Declan made a restive movement in his chair, his dark brows flexed in query. 'How are your computer skills, Jodi? We'd need you to be able to collate information, get the patients' histories logged in and kept up to date.'

'I'm thoroughly computer literate.' Jodi twitched a long hank of dark hair over her shoulder. 'I work quickly and thoroughly and I'm quite aware of the confidential nature of the job here. I'll sign a clause to that effect if you need me to.'

Emma bit hard on the inside of her cheek to stop the grin that threatened. This kid was something else. 'We'll probably get round to that, Jodi. But, if Dr O'Malley agrees, I think we can offer you the job. Declan?'

'Uh—' Declan's eyes looked slightly glazed. He rocked forward in his chair. 'Let's agree on a trial period, Jodi, if that suits—say a month? And we'll see how things are going then?'

'Absolutely.' Jodi shrugged slender shoulders. Bending down, she flipped open her satchel. 'I'll leave you my CV. And there are several character references as well.' She placed the file on the desk. 'If there's anything else you need to know, I'll be available on my mobile.' She smiled confidently and whirled to her feet. 'So, I'll see you both on Monday, then.'

'Good grief,' Declan said faintly after Jodi had swished out of the door. 'Do you get the feeling *we're* the ones who have just been interviewed?'

Emma chuckled. 'It's the Gen Y thing. They're

inclined to set out terms and conditions to prospective employers. But isn't she marvellous?'

'Made me feel about a hundred and six,' Declan growled. 'Hell, was I ever that young and enthusiastic about life?'

Emma stood and pushed her chair back in. 'Probably we both were.'

'Mmm.' Declan's tone was non-committal. 'Well, we seem to have made a dint in what needs to be done here so, if you're ready, I'd like to see over your hospital.'

CHAPTER THREE

BENDEMERE'S hospital was old but beautifully kept. Declan looked around with growing interest. 'This place has a long history, obviously,' he remarked.

'My grandfather actually funded the building of it,' Emma said proudly. 'These days, much of the accommodation is given over to nursing home beds for our seniors. Anything acute is sent straight on to Toowoomba by road ambulance. Or, in the case of serious trauma, we stabilise as best we can and chopper the patient out to Brisbane.'

'Do you have a theatre?' Declan began striding ahead, his interest clearly raised.

'A small one—just here.' She turned into an annexe and indicated the big oval window that looked into the pristine operating space. 'Dad did basic surgical procedures. And Rachel Wallace, our nurse manager, has extensive theatre experience. She insists the maintenance is kept up. Shame it's not used any more...'

'It's all here though, isn't it?' Declan's gaze

roamed almost hungrily, left and right and back again, as if to better acquaint himself with the layout. 'Who did the gas when your dad operated?'

'Oliver Shackelton. He's retired in the district. And, even though he won't see seventy again, I know Dad trusted his skills to the nth degree.'

'Interesting.' Declan pressed his lips together and took a deep breath. This was his natural environment. But he didn't belong here any longer. Suddenly, it all came at him in a rush, a heartbeat, the past coming forward to link with the present. He felt the sudden tightening of his throat muscles. It was over. He was finished as a surgeon. He couldn't operate any more. At least not in any way that was meaningful—from his standpoint, at least...

'Declan...are you OK?'

Declan's head came up, looking at her without seeing. 'Sorry?'

'We should get on,' she cajoled gently.

'Yes, we should.' He turned abruptly, as if to shut out the scene he'd walked into so unguardedly. He felt weird, in no way prepared for the hollow feeling in his gut as he snapped off the light and closed the double doors on the annexe.

Emma's gaze moved over him. 'Sure you're OK?'

He saw the compassion in her eyes, the softening, felt her empathy. But he wasn't a kid who needed to cry on her shoulder. 'I'm fine,' he said, his tone gruff as if brushing her concern aside. 'Fill me in about hospital staff.'

Emma gave a mental shrug. He hadn't fooled her for a minute. Well, if that was how he wanted to handle it, that was his business, his life. 'I've sent out an email to the nurses to advise them you were joining the practice.' She didn't add they'd probably done their own research on the Internet in the meantime. 'Rachel is our nurse manager,' she reiterated as they made their way along to the station. 'We have three other permanent RNs who alternate shifts and Dot Chalmers is permanent nights. Ancillary staff are rostered as necessary.'

'Leave and sick days?' Declan fell into step beside her.

'Covered by a small pool of nurses who mainly live in the district.'

'That seems like a reasonable set-up,' Declan said. 'I imagine the staff value their jobs quite highly.'

'And the folk hereabouts value *them*,' Emma said, leaving him in no doubt that any changes there would be unacceptable. Just in case he was thinking along those lines.

'Hospital maintenance is covered by a local firm,

as is security. And Betty Miller is our indispens-
able hospital cook.'

Declan nodded, taking everything on board. He
began to quicken his pace.

'Patients now?'

Emma rolled her eyes. He'd have to learn to
slow down if he was going to relate to the locals.
'Is there a fire somewhere?' she enquired innocently.

'Forgot.' He sent her a twisted grin. 'I'm keen
to get cracking, that's all.'

'Hello, people.' Rachel, tall and slender, came
towards them, her nimbus of auburn hair stark
against the white walls of the hospital corridor.
'And you are Dr O'Malley, I presume?' Beaming,
the nurse manager stuck her hand out towards
Declan.

'I am.' Declan shook her hand warmly. 'And it's
Declan. I've just been getting the lay of the land
from Emma. It looks like a great little hospital.'

'We're proud of it.' Rachel spun her gaze between the two medical officers. 'Um—I was just
on my way for a cuppa.'

'Don't let us hold you up,' Emma insisted.
Despite it being a small hospital, she knew the
nurses worked hard and deserved their breaks.

'OK, then. I won't be long.' Rachel began to
move away and then turned back. 'I knew you'd

be along so I've pulled the charts on our current patients.'

'Take your time.' Emma smiled. 'And thanks, Rach. We'll be fine.'

'I guess you know this place like the back of your hand,' Declan surmised as they made their way along to the nurses' station.

Emma sent him a quick look. It still seemed surreal that this once highly ambitious, powerful man was now to all intents and purposes her practice partner. Her hand closed around the small medallion at her throat. No doubt, for the moment, the newness of what he'd taken on was enough to keep him motivated. But what would happen when the grind of family practice began to wear thin? Where would his motivation be then?

In a dry little twist of quirky humour, Emma transposed the scenario into equine terms. Surely what Declan was proposing was like expecting a thoroughbred racer to feel fulfilled pulling a plough...

'Something amusing you, Emma?' Declan lifted a dark brow.

'Not really,' she said, going behind the counter and collecting the charts Rachel had left out.

'OK, who's the first cab off the rank?' Declan asked, settling on one of the high stools next to her.

'Russell Kernow, age seventy-five, lives alone,' Emma said. 'I saw him at the surgery a week ago. He was presenting with an incessant cough, raised temperature. I prescribed roxithromycin. His condition didn't improve and I admitted him two days ago. He was seriously dehydrated, complained his chest felt tight. I've placed him on an inhaler twice daily and the cough seems to have diminished slightly. I've sent bloods off as well.'

'So, you're testing for what—serology, pertussis, mycoplasma?'

'Plus legionella,' Emma said.

Declan raised a dark brow. 'Is that a possibility?'

'A remote one, but Russell's house is fully airconditioned. He spends much of his time indoors. And we've since found out the filters on his aircon unit haven't been changed for two years.'

'Still…legionella is drawing a fairly long bow,' Declan considered.

Emma bristled. If he was going to start telling her her job, they were going to fall out before the ink was dry on their partnership papers.

Their eyes met. He could see the spark of hostility in her gaze. Hell, he didn't want to blow things with her before they even got off the ground. 'Just thinking aloud,' he said hastily. 'It's your call. When do you expect the results?'

'Soonish,' Emma said, faintly mollified. 'I've requested the path lab to fax them to us here.' She turned, stroking a stray lock of hair behind her ear. 'Next patient is Sylvia Gartrell, age sixty-five. Recently had surgery—hysterectomy and bladder repair. Post-op seven days. The air ambulance delivered her to us yesterday.'

Declan ran his index finger between his brows. 'What's the problem?'

'Her bladder function hasn't yet returned to normal. She's having to self-catheterise and she's finding the procedure difficult to manage. Currently, the nurses are giving her some guidance. It seemed the safest option to have her here until she feels competent to go it alone. At the moment she's convinced she'll be stuck with this problem for ever so she needs emotional support as well.'

'Why was she released from hospital in the first place?'

Emma sighed. 'Same old story. They needed the bed.'

'Oh, for crying out loud! We'll need to keep a close eye on her, be mindful of the possibility of infection.'

'We're all aware of that, Declan.'

He sighed. 'OK, then, who's next on our patient list?'

'Only one more. Ashleigh Maine, aged eleven. Poor little kid had a bad asthma attack yesterday. Scared the life out of her.'

'So what's her prognosis?'

'She's getting some relief from a nebuliser and of course she's on a drip. Her home situation is not as good as it could be, though. Dad still smokes.'

Declan swore under his breath. 'I realize tobacco is the drug some folk cling to when they're under stress but surely, if his child is suffering, the man has to take stock of his actions?'

'Normally, Ashleigh's condition is fairly well managed but it only needs a change in routine and she's struggling again.'

'Are you aware of the study on asthmatics that's been carried by the Jarvis Institute in Sydney?' Declan asked pointedly.

Emma's gaze was suddenly uncertain. 'It's a breathing technique, isn't it? I think there's a new physio in Toowoomba who's a graduate from the Institute. We got some leaflets. I was going to investigate it further just before Dad…died. Do you want to take the child on to your list?'

'Fine with me,' he replied calmly. 'I'll chase up the physio and get the parents in for a round-table chat. I've a few ideas that might help as well.'

Emma defended her corner quietly. 'I did try to put the parents in touch with the Asthma

Foundation. They run camps and things that Ashleigh could attend with other youngsters with the same health problem. They declined.'

Declan's response was swift. 'Leave it with me, Emma. I'm new to the place. They'll take notice, believe me.'

Emma opened her mouth and closed it. She hoped he wouldn't jump all over the family. It wasn't the way things worked in rural medicine. If the Maines took offence, that would be the end of the doctors getting access to Ashleigh. Oh, help. Which way should she jump? Forward, if she had any sense. 'You will tread gently, won't you, Declan?'

His jaw hardened. 'I'll do what I need to do, Emma.'

'Not with my patients, you won't,' she flared. 'Bendemere is a close-knit community. You can't go around upsetting people.'

Hell, this was a minefield. She was guarding her territory, whereas he was used to giving orders and having them carried out immediately. OK, then. Back off, he told himself. 'If we want this partnership to work, Emma, we have to trust each other's medical skills. You haven't had any complaints about my patient contact, have you?'

'No...' She lifted her hands in appeasement.

'It's just— we're not used to working with each other yet.'

His mouth pulled tight. Was this what he was about to sign on for—bickering over someone who couldn't grasp that his inability to quit smoking was stuffing up his child's health? He lifted his gaze to glance meaningfully at her. 'Just let's try to keep it professional, then.'

Emma gritted her teeth. That was a low blow. She'd done everything she could under very difficult circumstances to keep their relationship professional. He'd been the one to overstep this morning when he'd touched her cheek! She tried to steady her thoughts. She'd have to swallow her angst with him if she didn't want everything turned into ashes. New jobs had been promised and already there was an air of expectation about the town. She breathed a sigh of relief when she saw Rachel heading towards them, a tea tray in her hands. 'I thought you might need this,' she said. 'And Betty's made us some of her special ginger biscuits,' she added brightly, sensing an air of tension between the two.

'Lovely,' Emma said faintly.

'I'll take a rain check, thanks, Rachel.' Declan spun off his stool. 'I'll get on and make myself known to our patients.'

'Then I'll accompany you,' Rachel said.

'There's no need.' He gave an impatient twitch of his shoulder. 'I'm sure I can manage.'

Rachel's raised brows spoke volumes, before she swept up the patient charts. 'My hospital, my call, Dr O'Malley. Besides, I need to strut my stuff occasionally,' she said cheekily. 'It's ages since I walked the wards with a posh doc.'

Emma watched them walk away together, saw Declan turn his head, heard his rumble of laughter as he interacted with Rachel. She made a little sniff of disapproval. Shaking off a disquiet she didn't understand, she took up one of Betty's ginger biscuits and dunked it in her tea.

By Sunday afternoon Emma was going stir-crazy. It wasn't that she didn't have a million things she could be doing. She just couldn't settle to anything. Declan had offered to be on call for the weekend so that had left her with more free time than she'd had in months. She'd done a tour of the garden and picked a bunch of winter roses to bring some warmth and friendliness to reception. At least Moira would appreciate her gesture. She doubted Declan would even notice.

She was back to *him* again. She still had the feeling of things being not quite right between them. He'd erupted into the practice and into her life and she'd hardly had time to take stock. He hadn't exactly steamrollered over her but he hadn't wasted any time in putting his plans into action. But then she'd given him tacit permission, hadn't she? Because the alternative had been too bleak to contemplate.

Oh, help. Emma turned her restless gaze towards the kitchen window. It would be dark soon. Suddenly she was beset with a strange unease. She couldn't begin the first week of their new partnership with so many of her questions unresolved.

They needed to talk.

Now she'd decided, she wouldn't hold back, although her heart was slamming at the thought of what she was about to take on. They'd already exchanged mobile phone numbers. She'd find him about the place somewhere.

He answered on the fourth ring. 'O'Malley.'

'Hi—it's me—Emma.'

'Problem?'

She took a shallow breath. He wasn't making this easy. 'Are you busy?'

'Er—no. I've just been for a jog.'

Emma blinked uncertainly. 'How did it go?'

'Pretty good,' he said, sounding pleased with himself. 'What's up?'

'Nothing, really. I wondered whether we could get together this evening—just sort out a few things before work tomorrow...'

'OK...' He seemed to be thinking. 'Want to grab a bite to eat somewhere, then? Or, better still, come to me. I've moved into the log cabin at Foley's farm. Know where it is?'

'Yes.' Emma's fingers tightened on the phone. The Foleys lived about a kilometre out of town. 'I thought it was only a holiday let.'

'I struck a deal with the Foleys. It's mine for as long as I need it.'

'I see...well, that's good. About dinner—I've made soup. I could bring some over.'

He curled a low laugh. 'You're obviously intent on feeding me. But soup sounds good. I did a shop this morning. I'm sure we'll find something to go with it.'

Declan felt a new spring in his step as he threw himself under the shower. How odd that Emma must have been thinking about him just at the same moment he'd been thinking about her...

Emma was glad he'd found somewhere to live, and the log cabin was a comfortable option for the time being, she thought, guiding the car carefully over the cattle grid that marked the entrance to the farm. The cabin was barely five minutes drive further on and in seconds she saw the lighted windows come into view. As she pulled to a stop in front of the cabin, her heart began its pattering again, the nerves in her stomach lurching and flailing like a drunken butterfly.

Out of the car, she took a moment to look up at the sky. It was the same night sky she'd been seeing since she was a child, the same stars. But tonight she noticed them in a way she never had before. The Milky Way was its usual wash of grey-white light, peppered with twinkling stars. But tonight, as she watched, one lone star shot across the heavens, leaving a glittering trail of light before it disappeared.

'Stargazing?' Declan's deep voice was husky behind her.

'Oh—' Emma spun round, giving a jagged half-laugh. He was standing on the sheltered front porch. 'I didn't know you were there.'

'Saw your headlights. Coming in?'

'Mmm.' Suddenly, for no reason at all, anticipation was a sweet ache in her chest, a flutter in her breathing. She held her vacuum jug of soup tightly and followed him inside.

The cabin was open-plan and modern with the lounge area and kitchen melded into one living space. 'Oh, good,' Emma said lightly. 'You've got the fire going.'

'Glass of wine?' Declan offered as they moved across the timber floor to the kitchen. 'I have a nice local red.'

'OK, thanks.' Emma placed her soup on the counter top. 'You should be comfortable here.'

Declan didn't comment. Instead, he took up the wine he'd left breathing and poured two glasses. He handed one to Emma, unable to stop himself gazing at her with an intensity that made his heart stall for a second and then pick up speed. She was wearing jeans that clung to her legs and outlined a pert little backside. Her top was a frilly button-up shirt, the neckline open just enough to expose a hint of cleavage. Her hair had a just-washed, just-brushed shine about it and when their gazes met and she smiled at him he felt a jolt to every one of his senses. Hell. How was he going to get through the evening without wanting to…?

'What?' Emma raised a quick brow.

He shrugged, breaking eye contact quickly. 'I guess we should drink to the future of our *partnership.*'

Emma's mind went blank. They seemed to have travelled half a lifetime in a few days. Even this morning, she'd woken with a start, wondering whether she'd dreamed it all—that she actually had a partner for the practice, someone to rely on, to confer with—to trust. 'I guess we should.' She gave a tinny laugh to disguise the sudden attack of nerves. Lifting her glass to his, she echoed, 'To our partnership.'

'What kind of soup did you bring?' Declan cringed at the banality of his conversation. But his brain felt like shredded cheese.

'Minestrone.'

'A meal in itself.' He sent her a crooked grin. 'I put some herb bread in the oven to warm when I knew you were bringing soup.'

Emma savoured another mouthful of the full-bodied wine. 'You know about food, then?'

He lifted a shoulder modestly. 'I went along to the farmers' market this morning. I thought I might have seen you there.'

Emma blinked rapidly. 'I used to go when I had time to cook.'

'The produce is amazing,' Declan said, indicating they should take their wine through to the lounge area. 'I couldn't stop buying stuff.'

Emma chuckled. 'And I'll bet the stall-holders couldn't wait to sell you *stuff.* The whole town will know who you are by now.'

'They will?' He looked startled.

'And that you're living here and fending for yourself.'

He groaned. 'It won't be daily casseroles at the surgery, will it?'

'Not just casseroles.' Emma sent him an innocent wide-eyed look and curled herself into the big squishy armchair. 'There'll possibly be apple pies as well. Bendemere will want you to feel at home here.'

'I think I'm beginning to already.' He'd taken his place on the sofa opposite her. 'By the way, I released young Ashleigh this afternoon.'

'Any problems?'

He was about to ask if she'd expected any. Except he'd seen the flash of worry in her eyes. 'None at all,' he elaborated. 'And I have Aaron and Renee coming in for a chat tomorrow.'

Emma felt a flood of relief. If he'd already got on first name terms with the Maines, then he must have at least listened to her concerns and trod softly. 'They're not bad parents. They're just—'

'Young?' Declan gave a rueful smile. 'I'll be gentle with them, Emma, but I promise I'll get through to them, whatever it takes.'

Well, she guessed she couldn't ask for more than that. She took another mouthful of wine and then leaned forward to place her glass on the coffee table between them. In a second her thoughts began racing like an out of control juggernaut. She'd come to ask Declan something. She tried to think of the best way to say what she'd come to say but, in the end, there was really no lead-in for the questions she needed answers to. 'Declan—' she paused and wet her lips, tasting the sweetness of the wine '—I need to run something past you.'

'About the practice?'

'No.' Emma swallowed hard. 'I want to know the extent of your involvement with my father.'

'I thought I'd told you.'

Not nearly enough. 'You mentioned Dad was your boss when you were at John Bosco's and that he took a special interest in you. Was there a reason for that? I mean, there must have been a large group of interns. Why did he single you out?'

So here it was, sooner than he would have liked. Deep down, he'd known someone as astute as Emma would not have been content with the glib kind of scenario he'd painted about knowing her father. Very deliberately, he took a mouthful of his wine and placed his glass next to hers on the coffee table. His jaw tightened. 'I was about ten, I suppose, when your dad started visiting our home.'

Emma stared at him uncertainly. 'Was someone ill?'

He shook his head. 'My mother was a nurse. She and Andrew worked together in Casualty at the Prince Alfred in Melbourne.'

Oh. She hadn't expected that. She quickly put dates and ages together in her head. Dad would have been married to Mum by then... 'What were the circumstances? How did——*why* did Dad become involved with your family?'

He looked at her steadily. 'Are you sure you want to hear this, Emma?'

Emma had no idea where their conversation was leading and her stomach was churning. But she knew she needed answers. 'Yes.'

He rocked his hand as if say, *so be it.* 'My parents, me and my two younger sisters were just a regular little family living in the suburbs of Melbourne when my dad was killed in an industrial accident. Suddenly our lives were turned upside down. Overnight, Mum was a sole supporting parent with three kids to feed and educate. She had no choice than to switch from part-time to full-time work.'

Emma shook her head. She'd been indulged as a child and had wanted for nothing in a material sense. 'It must have been very hard on you all.'

'No, not hard, exactly.' His mouth lifted in a token smile. 'Just different. I know I had to grow up pretty fast. Erinn and Katie were only little girls.'

'You had to be the man of the house.'

He shrugged. 'Mum worked an early shift. We went to a neighbour's until it was time for school and Mum was always home for us in the afternoon. We missed Dad, of course, were bewildered for a time. But, after a while, kids being kids, we accepted our lives as they were, changes and all. But I guess Mum had worries she never told us about. Well, how could she?' The muscle in his jaw kicked for a second. 'It was about that time Andrew began calling round. Mum merely said he was a friend from the hospital. Sometimes he brought groceries, had a kick of the football with me. He seemed to enjoy being around us kids. Told us he had a little girl called Emma.'

Emma licked lips that seemed bone-dry. 'H-how long did he keep coming to see you? Weeks, months…?'

'Couple of months, I guess. I was a kid, Emma. Time didn't mean much. I just remember when he stopped coming. I asked Mum about it. She said he'd left the PA and gone to another hospital. He wouldn't be able to see us any more.'

Emma lifted eyes that were wide and anguished. 'Do you think they were…*involved*?'

'I don't know,' he said evenly.

She swallowed hard, as if unable to voice the questions crowding her head. Had Dad fallen in love with—? 'What was your mother's name?' she asked.

'Anne,' Declan said quietly. 'She was called Anne. She died a couple of years ago.'

Anne O'Malley. The name sat frozen inside

Emma, along with a block of emotions. She'd never heard her father refer to anyone by that name. Never. But obviously Dad's involvement with Declan hadn't ended there. 'Was it pure chance you and Dad met up again when you were an intern?'

'It seemed like chance. Perhaps he'd simply seen my name on the intake list. I do know he was extremely interested in my welfare. But he was discreet. I never felt I was treated differently than the others. But I knew I could go to him with any problems.'

Emma smiled sadly. 'That sounds like Dad. But you mentioned wanting to chuck in medicine. Why was that?'

'My mother had a stroke...' Declan's words were drawn out softly, seeming to echo in the close confines of the cabin. 'She was only forty-eight. Both Erinn and Katie were at Uni. Money was tight. I figured I could get a *real* job, start bringing in the big bucks.' He rubbed at his jaw. 'God only knows what I thought I was capable of doing. When I told Andrew, he was shocked. He told me I had the potential to make a fine doctor.' Declan gave a rough laugh. 'At the time I remember wondering how *potential* was going to pay the bills. Mum's rehab was dragging on and I knew it would be a long time before she could work again—if ever.

Then, suddenly out of the blue, she was whisked off to a private clinic with the latest methods. I gathered Andrew had arranged it. I have the feeling he paid for it as well.'

Emma just nodded. If she'd had any doubts before, then she had none now. Dad had fallen in love with Anne but he'd stayed with his wife. *For my sake?* she wondered now. Or maybe Anne had sent him away so as not to break up his family. They'd never know. Emma was not about to ask her own mother. Ever. Sometimes, it was better not to revisit old wounds, old memories.

Somehow, they got through the rest of the evening. They ate their soup and the warmed herb bread and made desultory conversation.

'What made you decide to go for a jog?' Emma asked later, washing the platter they'd used for the local cheeses and crisp slices of apple they'd eaten instead of dessert.

'I went out on to the porch, took one look at the paddock and all that space and thought, why not?'

'And it was good?'

'It was fine,' he hedged. He didn't tell her he'd begun to ache all over. He felt almost relieved when Emma glanced surreptitiously at her watch.

The evening had strained them both. 'Cup of tea before you go?'

'No, I won't, thanks,' she said almost hurriedly. 'I'll just grab my Thermos jug.'

Declan managed a quick smile. 'I'll walk you out.'

'Thanks.' Emma's return smile was edged with vulnerability.

On the lighted porch, Declan paused and looked down at her. 'Are you OK?'

'You've given me a bit to think about.'

His mouth drew in. She'd sounded shaky and the eyes that lifted briefly to his were guarded and shadowed. Almost in slow motion, he took the Thermos from her unprotesting hands and set it on the outdoor table. 'Come here...'

Emma fought a losing battle as he gathered her close. Every caressing detail of his hands was conveyed to her through the thin stuff of her shirt, lapping at the edge of her resistance. Confusion and need struggled for supremacy.

'Half-truths wouldn't have done,' he said quietly.

'I know,' she said huskily, not trusting her voice too far.

Declan frowned down at her. A tiny chill wind had come in a flurry behind her, separating tendrils of her hair from around her face and fluffing them out. For an instant, she'd looked so young. And so alone.

'It's just—I don't quite know where I fit any more,' she said quietly, an admission that was heightened by her evident uncertainty about *what* to think.

'You were the sunshine of your father's life, Emma. Hell, you must know he'd have moved mountains for you?'

Her mouth trembled. 'Perhaps he was just over-compensating. Perhaps he felt guilty that he'd rather have been with Anne and all of you.'

Declan swore under his breath. 'That's rubbish. Did you ever feel second-best?'

She shook her head. 'It's been a bit of a revelation all the same. About Dad.'

'With hindsight, would you have rather stayed in ignorance?'

Letting her breath go on a heavy sigh, she stepped away from the weight of his hands.'I honestly don't know.'

CHAPTER FOUR

DECLAN immersed himself in his Monday morning surgery. It was better he did, he thought, grabbing a quick coffee between patients. Anything to keep his mind from flipping back to last night and Emma's reaction to what he'd told her. Now he wondered whether he'd done the right thing in telling her anything.

He could have pleaded ignorance. But secrets had a way of surfacing when you least expected. And, in reality, did any of it matter now? Emma seemed to think so. He sighed and reached for his phone when it rang softly. 'Yes, Moira?'

'Your eleven o'clock's cancelled, Declan, and the Maines are here already.'

'OK, I'll come out. And don't forget I'm going to need extra time for this consult, Moira.'

'All taken care of.'

'Thanks.' He replaced the handpiece and got to his feet. Moments later, he was ushering Aaron and Renee Maine through to his office. When they were settled, he said, 'Just for the record, you're not on trial here. But obviously I need your input if we're to sort something out for Ashleigh. Do you have any idea what may have triggered her asthma this time?'

'She had a cold.' Renee kept her gaze averted. 'Sometimes, no matter what we do, she can't seem to throw it off.'

'I know my smoking doesn't help...' Aaron came in. He paused and chewed his bottom lip. 'Renee and me have talked a bit—' He stretched out his hands, his knuckles white as he clasped them across his jeans-clad thighs. 'I reckon I have to quit. And no mucking about this time.'

'Well, that's very good news.' Declan leaned forward earnestly. 'There's a great deal of help I can give you for that.'

Aaron shook his head. 'I'm gonna chuck out my cigarettes—go cold turkey.'

'That's pretty drastic, Aaron.' Declan was cautious. 'And I'd like to give you a physical before you start, if that's OK?'

'Yeah, whatever. I just want the poison outta me system.'

'Dr O'Malley—' Renee paused, nervously winding a strand of dark hair around her finger '—could you explain just what happens when Ashleigh gets an attack? This time, it scared us spitless. We had to call the ambulance.'

'Sure.' Declan swung round to the bank of filing cabinets behind him. 'I actually put together some reading matter for you.' He pulled out a file and opened it. 'There's a chart here that will give you an idea of the body's reaction during an asthma attack.' So saying, he flipped out the chart and placed it in front of the young parents. 'As you know, asthma affects the lungs,' he explained. 'When someone experiences an attack the tubes begin narrowing, making breathing difficult.'

'Oh—that's the wheezing sound Ashleigh makes?' Renee looked at Declan fearfully, fisting her hands and crossing them over her chest.

Almost an hour later, during which Declan had drawn diagrams for the parents and explained in depth the crippling effects of an asthma attack on their daughter, Renee said, 'I feel like we're really getting somewhere at last. And we'll need to go to the physio's appointment with Ashleigh, then?'

'It's essential.' Declan was unequivocal. 'One of you should be there and learn the breathing technique with your daughter.'

'We can do that.' Renee's mouth trembled into a shaky smile. 'We're ever so grateful to you for explaining everything. Thank you, Dr O'Malley.'

'Yeah. Thanks, Doc,' Aaron said awkwardly. 'Thanks a lot.'

'Ashleigh's a great kid,' Declan complimented them. 'Take care of her.'

'Oh, we will.' Renee linked hands with her husband and they stood together.

'Er—when do you want me for this medical, Doc?' Aaron's chin came up and his shoulders straightened as if he'd at last taken charge of his life and his family.

'The sooner, the better.' Declan opened the door of his consulting room for them. 'Sort out something with Moira as you leave.'

Emma was in some kind of shock. She knew the signs and she also knew it would pass. But finding out about Dad… Clicking off her computer, she got to her feet. Possibly, it had had the same impact as finding out as an adult that you were adopted.

But she and Declan had got through the first week as practice partners without any major dramas. She should be glad about that. Not that they'd seen much of one another. Well, not for long enough to have talked about anything other than the patients. Now it was Friday and they were about to begin their first staff meeting. Moira had been invited to attend.

'Let's keep this as brief and to the point as we

can,' Declan suggested as they sat at the table in the staffroom.

'I don't have any complaints,' Moira said in her forthright style.

'How's Jodi shaping up?' Declan flipped his pen back and forth between his fingers.

'Very well,' Emma came in. 'She's caught on exactly to what we need.'

'Good.' Declan turned to face Emma. 'Libby still OK to start with us on Monday?'

'She can do a four-day week,' Emma said. 'If we're happy to work around that?'

'Fine with me,' Declan said economically.

'Libby's coming in for some orientation to-morrow,' Emma relayed. 'She and I will go over things so she's up to speed and then she'll start officially on Monday—if that's all right with you, Declan?'

'Sounds very proactive. And make sure we pay Libby for the Saturday hours, please, Moira.' He lifted his head and raised an eyebrow between the two women. 'If that's all the staff business, then?'

'I've nothing else,' Moira said.

'Nor me.' Emma shook her head.

'Right.' Declan scooted his chair back from the table and stretched out his legs. 'Moira, feel free to take off, then. And thanks for making my first week such a smooth ride.'

'Oh—how nice of you to say so, Declan,' Moira responded coyly. 'I think we're going to make a great team.' She stood to her feet, sending the two doctors a broad smile. 'See you both on Monday.'

'Have a nice weekend,' they chorused.

Moira was barely out of the door when Declan rounded on Emma. 'Any patients you want to consult about?'

'A couple.' She gave an inward shrug. Did he always conduct his meetings at this pace? 'The lab confirmed Russell Kernow has whooping cough.'

'Poor old boy! Probably jabs for that weren't around when he was a kid. Not much we can do, though. It will just have to run its course. And the good thing is he's not infectious any longer. So, you'll release him then?'

Emma nodded. 'From a funding point of view, we can't justify keeping him indefinitely. Someone from the Rotary has been round to his home and replaced the filters in his air-con units and the meals on wheels will start calling again.'

Declan ran a finger across his chin thoughtfully. 'We should probably keep up a regular home visit, though.'

'I'll tee up with Libby to pop in on him each day. Anything untoward, she can report to us,' Emma said.

'Great.' Declan smiled and raised his arms and locked them at the back of his neck. 'How about your gynae patient, Sylvia?'

Emma was surprised he'd remembered such a small detail as a patient's first name. 'She's gone home. Her bladder function is still incomplete but she's managing much better. Her husband is at home for support and I aim to see her regularly until everything is back to normal. How was your consult with the Maines?' Emma pressed back a strand of hair behind her ear, shifting the angle of her gaze to look fully at him.

'Er—productive, I think.' Declan caught the concentration of her gaze, noting how the forest-green of her eyes was unusually dark, her expression almost wistful. His heart thumped, the memory of her feminine softness under his hands making his body tighten uncomfortably. Hell...he was almost tempted to cancel his plans for the weekend. And do what? the practical part of his brain demanded.

'And?' Her mouth was smiling. Just. More a tiny upward flick at the corners. 'Wakey, wakey, Doctor.'

'Huh!' Declan gave a crack of laughter. 'Slipped

out of focus there for a minute. What were we talking about?'

'The Maine family.'

'Right.' He spun a finger up in comprehension. 'Aaron is chucking the smokes and Ashleigh is booked to see the physio next week. All on the file.' He cranked a dark eyebrow at her. 'You all set to cover for the weekend?'

She nodded.

'Good. Looks like we can wrap it up, then.' He clicked his pen closed and pushed it back in his shirt pocket. 'I'll just grab my bag and be off.' In one fluid movement, he'd stood to his feet and pushed his chair in.

Somewhat more slowly, Emma followed suit. She caught up with him again as he came out of his office, pulling the door closed and locking it. 'You seem in an almighty hurry to get out of the place.' Emma tried to dismiss the odd stab of disappointment she felt, almost running to keep up with him as he strode back out to reception.

'I'm driving to Brisbane.' Declan hoisted his medical case on to the counter top and wheeled to face her. 'Erinn is flying in for a conference. It's been ages since we've been able to catch up.'

'No wonder you're excited, then.' Emma managed a quick smile. 'So, what kind of conference is it?'

'Erinn is an OT,' he said, as if that would explain everything.

Emma blinked. An occupational therapist. 'And Katie? What does she do?' Emma knew she was holding him up but suddenly, for reasons she didn't want to analyse, she needed to put him together with his family. See them as a unit. Something *she* didn't have any longer.

'Katie teaches high school. Year eights. The *littlies,* as she calls them. Loves it.'

He laughed and then drawled sing-song, 'And they're both married to good guys and both have two kids each.'

Emma wrinkled her nose at him. 'So why aren't *you* married?' she asked lightly.

'Dunno. Never happened.' Raising an arm, he flipped his case off the counter top. 'Er...if there's a crisis of any kind—call me,' he instructed. 'I'll come galloping back.'

Her laugh cracked in the middle. 'On your white charger?'

'You bet. Isn't that what knights do?'

'Very cute.' Head thrown back, Emma caught his gaze. Her smile widened. Declan smiled back and, for just a moment, a blink of time, there was a connection of shared awareness. Sharp. Intense. Then, suddenly, their smiles retracted as quickly as turning off a light switch.

They both looked awkwardly away at precisely the same moment. And Declan was gone in the time it took for him to stride down the ramp to the parking area at the front of the surgery and cross to his car.

Against her better judgement, Emma watched from the window. In seconds he'd taken off, the bonnet of his silver-grey Audi a flash in the setting sun as he passed the border of flowering plumbago and was lost to sight. Emma stifled a sigh and drew back. He was on his way.

Suddenly all the places in her heart felt empty.

A peculiar kind of separateness engulfed her. She had nowhere to go.

And she realized she'd wanted to go with Declan. Be close with him. Meet his sister. Gather the warmth of family about her. *Oh, dear God.* Lifting a hand, she pressed it against her mouth. Where did she think she was going with any of this?

She needed to get a serious grip.

Keep busy. That was the best option. The only option. She locked up and set the alarm and then looked at her watch. It was still relatively early. She had time to pop in on Sylvia.

'How is everything going?' Emma asked as they sat side by side in the Gartrells' comfortable lounge room.

The older woman smiled. 'Tom's treating me

like a queen. Doing the washing and everything. And we do the cooking together.'

'You know not to lift heavy pots and things,' Emma warned.

Sylvia flicked her hand dismissively. 'I just give the orders and Tom takes direction. We're quite a team.'

Emma chuckled. 'I'm sure you are. Now, how about the rest of you?'

Sylvia leaned forward confidentially. 'I think I may have had a breakthrough with the water. It's coming much better.'

'That's brilliant, Sylvia. You're still measuring the output?'

'Like you told me.'

'And how much are you still retaining?'

Sylvia thought for a second. 'About fifty mils. And I used the catheter to get that away. But I must say it's getting a bit tiresome.'

'Well, I think you can stop, now.'

'I can? Really?'

'Yes. Most of us retain that amount of urine naturally. I'd say nature's taken over and your body is well on the way to a complete recovery.'

'Oh, my!' Sylvia's hand went to her chest. 'You know I thought it would never happen. Even turn-ing on the water at the basin like the nurses said didn't help. I was beginning to think I was some kind of oddity.'

'Oh, Sylvia, of course you're not! It's been a struggle but you'll reap the rewards of having the surgery done now.'

'Yes. And now I can power on again, get into my garden and help with the grandkids much more.'

'But not for a while yet,' Emma cautioned. 'You've had major surgery, Sylvia. Now, barring emergencies, could you come and see me in two weeks and we'll check everything is where it should be?'

'I can do that, dear.'

'About medication…' Emma flipped open the file she'd brought with her. 'I'd like you to stay on the hormone cream the specialist prescribed. Do you have enough for the next two weeks? If not, I'll write you a new script.'

'I have one repeat left,' Sylvia said. 'That nice new partner you have wrote me a script when he popped in on me at the hospital.'

'Oh—' Emma frowned. That would have been on that Saturday morning when they'd only just firmed up their partnership. But there was nothing on file… She lowered her gaze and rechecked the information. Oh, yes—there it was, in Declan's precise handwriting. So, why hadn't she seen it? She bit her lip thoughtfully. Probably because she hadn't been looking for it. Hadn't expected Declan to have become involved so quickly in a hands-on kind of way with their patients. She blinked a bit, not quite able to admit that she was missing the solidarity of his presence already.

Emma got to her feet. 'I'll see myself out, Sylvia. Don't get up.'

'Tom should be back any minute,' Sylvia said. 'He's just gone to get our usual Friday fish and chips for tea. Why don't you stay, dear? He always buys extra.' A grin tweaked a dimple in her cheek. 'Still can't get used to the fact there's only the two of us now. Stay,' she invited again.

Emma was tempted. Lord, how she was tempted. The need to be with family, surrogate as it was, was almost unbearable. But, in reality, it would solve nothing. 'It's a lovely thought, Sylvia. And thanks. But...er...I've another patient I need to catch up with,' she invented hurriedly.

Sylvia nodded. 'Another time, then. And Emma?' Reaching up from her sitting position, the older woman squeezed the tips of Emma's fingers. 'Be kind to yourself, dear. Your dad would have wanted that for you.'

CHAPTER FIVE

HE WAS back.

Declan blew out a calming breath and switched off the ignition. He'd made good time from Brisbane and driven straight to Kingsholme, telling himself if Emma was out it was no big deal.

He stretched, felt a crack or two in his spine and shoulder joints, shrugged inwardly and swung out of the car. He'd go round to the back of the house. If the kitchen door was open, he'd know Emma was home.

Oh, hell. He worked his legs as he walked along the path at the side of the house. His joints felt as stiff and rusty as the Tin Man from *The Wizard of Oz*. Mounting the shallow steps to the verandah, he stood, quietly absorbing his surroundings.

It was a typical back verandah found in countless rural settings in Australia. A mish-mash of everyday items, from the outdoor shoes left to dry to the weathered wooden ladder that was being used as a plant stand. Two lovely old wicker chairs painted a silvery-blue were parked against the wall and in between sat a matching round wicker table covered with a patchwork cloth. On the table sat a little tea tray, a cup and saucer and a glass jar of...what? Shortbread? Something like that...

Declan took a hard breath and tunnelled a hand back through his hair. There was an odd feeling about the setting. A loneliness. Emma? His heart twisted. He hated that conclusion.

Moving purposefully across the verandah, he called a greeting from the open kitchen doorway. And waited, his heart banging like a drumbeat in his chest. There was no reply. Yet he knew she was here. He could *feel* it.

Warily, he took a couple of steps into the kitchen and looked around, his eyes widening, his face working at the sweetness of what he saw.

Emma was lying curled on the cane settee. It was obvious she was asleep, her pose unconsciously sexy yet vulnerable. Desire and need slammed into him with the intensity of a punch to the solar plexus, dizzying, like sudden gravity after weightlessness.

He felt a hard wedge in the region of his stomach and his jaw clenched. Oh, sweet heaven. This felt almost like voyeurism. Swallowing the dryness in his throat, he moved closer. 'Emma...'

His voice seemed to fall on Emma's skin like a caress, easing her out of sleep into wakefulness.

'Declan?' Her eyes shot open, her voice foggy with confusion. She jack-knifed to a sitting position. 'How long have you been there?'

'Just arrived. I didn't mean to intrude. Your kitchen door was open—'

'It's OK.' She lifted her hands, sweeping her hair back behind her ears. She gave a husky laugh. 'I started reading—must have fallen asleep.'

He frowned. 'Do you do that often—leave your door open? I could have been a burglar.'

She sent him a weighted look. 'What were you intending to steal—the kitchen chairs? The cat? This is a country town, Declan. No one locks their back doors.'

His mouth grew taut. 'I was concerned for you, that's all.'

Soft colour licked along Emma's cheekbones and she protested gruffly, 'Well, as you can see, I'm fine.' She stood to her feet. 'I thought you'd be back much later than this.'

Declan gave a twitch of his shoulder. 'Erinn's conference broke up at lunchtime. We both took off soon after. How was *your* weekend?'

Lonely without you, she was tempted to reply. But quickly thought better of it. 'Couple of call-outs,' she said. 'Nothing serious. So you had a good time with your sister?'

'Yes,' he said economically. 'Erinn and I had a few laughs, caught up on the family news.'

'As you do. Something to drink?' she asked, moving to the fridge, opening the door and peering into the contents, trying in vain to stem the smile that just wouldn't go away. He was back and somehow, in some odd way, her world felt right again. Which was crazy, she decided, leaning in to extract pear juice, a ginger cordial and soda water. She spun round and moved back to the bench. 'You'll like this,' she said, expertly mixing the three ingredients and then pouring the finished product into two tall glasses. She topped each glass with a sprig of mint and passed one across to Declan. 'It's delicious,' she promised when he hesitated over a taste test.

He held the glass to his lips and tasted once and then again, licking the residue from his lips. 'It's good,' he agreed and drank thirstily.

'Let's catch the last of the rays,' Emma invited, putting her own half-finished drink aside and leading the way out on to the verandah.

Ignoring the outdoor chairs, Declan moved to stand with his back against the railings. 'I'm a bit stiff after the drive,' he explained.

'So, was the trip back all right, then?' she asked, her hip almost touching his as she stood beside him.

'Mmm.' Why on earth were they talking such generalities? Stuff it. He couldn't hold back any longer. He turned to face her. 'I thought about you a lot over the weekend...'

Emma swallowed. Her heart tripped. He was bending towards her, his blue eyes capturing hers with an almost magnetic pull. 'I...'

'Thought about me too?' he murmured hopefully.

She had. She couldn't deny it. But would it help either of them if she told him that? Did she need the complication an admission would undoubtedly bring? She felt her heart bang out of rhythm, her gaze moving restlessly, almost fearfully, as though to find a way out of the dilemma.

The late afternoon sun felt intoxicatingly warm against her back. There was no urgency in the air. Just a languid kind of sweetness.

Declan leaned closer to her, slowly.

In a second, Emma felt her body trembling from the inside out. Was this what it felt like before a first kiss? Her mind went blank. After Marcus had defected, she'd thought she'd never again trust a man enough to experience another *first kiss*.

But she wanted it. How she wanted it.

Declan was so close to her now she could see the faint shadow across his jaw line, the slight smudges under his eyes. His face reflected a toughness, a strength.

'Emma...' he said, his voice low, this last second before his kiss.

Her mouth trembled. She could feel his breath on her face. It smelled minty, a faint residue from his drink. She lifted her gaze and stared at him, mesmerized by the yearning she saw in his eyes. The desire to be kissed by him was irresistible and, before she could second-guess the wisdom of it all, she was leaning into him.

Declan took her face in his hands, his need materialising in the softest sigh, before his mouth found hers. The kiss rolled through his blood and raw need slammed into him like nothing he had ever known before. Her lips parted and her own longing seemed to match his, overwhelming him like the heady aroma of some dark heated wine.

Applying a barely-there pressure through his hands, he whispered the tips of his fingers down the sides of her throat, then in a sweep across her breastbone to her shoulders, gathering her in.

Emma clung to him. And the kiss deepened, turned wrenching and wild. She felt a need inside her, an overwhelming need to be touched like this, held like this.

And *stroked* to the point of ecstasy by this man.

But it wasn't going to go that far. At least not

today. She felt Declan pulling back, breaking the kiss, slowly, gently, his lips leaving a shivering sweetness like trails of insubstantial gossamer.

A long beat of silence while they collected themselves.

'Have we broken every rule in the official partnership handbook?' Declan asked in a deep voice, wrapping her closer.

She licked her lips. 'Possibly…probably.'

He bent to her, pressing his forehead to hers. 'It's all been a bit…'

'Unexpected?' Emma was dizzy with the newness of it all.

'Huge understatement,' he declared. 'Bone-rattling would be more apt. Ah, Emma…' His fingers lifted her chin, his mouth only a breath away as he said her name and then his lips were on hers. Again. And it felt so right the second time around. To taste slowly and blissfully instead of devouring as if there were no tomorrow.

Emma felt intoxicated, as though she were swimming through warm treacle toffee, loving the vital male taste of him, the warmth of his arms around her, the long, slow getting-to-know-you kind of kiss that she guessed neither of them wanted to end. Because then there would be questions, post-mortems.

And no answers.

But of course the kiss had to end. Good things, unexpected pleasurable things, always did. This time at Emma's instigation. Slowly, she pulled back, untwining his arms from where he'd looped them around her shoulders and took a decisive step away from him.

Declan's shoulders lifted in a huge sigh. 'I guess I should go,' he murmured and hesitated. Then, as if still compelled to touch her, he reached for her, running his hands down her arms, lacing his fingers with hers. 'Before we get into any more trouble,' he added wryly, placing the softest kiss at the side of her mouth. 'See you tomorrow.' He let her go abruptly, turning away and making a swift exit across the verandah and down the steps to the path.

He didn't look back.

At work on Monday morning, Emma was still dazed by what had happened, her whole body still sensitized by Declan's kisses, her thoughts far from clear. She'd been woefully unprepared for the avalanche of emotions she'd felt—and never experienced before. Not even with Marcus, whom she'd almost married.

She went along to her consulting room, lifting a hand to touch the corner of her mouth where Declan had imprinted that last lingering kiss. He'd be arriving at the surgery very soon. Suddenly she felt fluttery, the expectation of seeing him intense, sizzling and her former safe world was spinning out of control.

Declan left the log cabin hardly noticing the chilly winter morning, still trying to untangle the strands of emotions inside him. He'd *kissed* Emma. God, how had he let that happen? He should have been concentrating on cementing their professional partnership, not reacting to his hormones like a randy adolescent.

But they'd only kissed, for crying out loud. People did that all the time. It didn't mean they were about to move in together! Emma would see it for what it was. Opportunity, time and place, the uniqueness of their circumstances and no doubt capped off by a build-up of emotional overload. He heaved in a controlling breath and concentrated on the road.

But, by the time he reached the surgery, the rationalisation he'd concocted was rapidly being drowned out by the clang of warning bells. He was kidding himself. It was nothing to do with hormones. It was about feelings. It was about Emma Armitage.

OK, play it by ear, Declan self-counselled as he made his way along the corridor to his consulting room. He stowed his medical case and straightened his shoulders. Moira had informed him Emma was already in. Closing the door to his surgery, he moved along to her room. Her door was slightly open. Nevertheless, he rapped before he went in. 'Morning.'

'Good morning.' Emma lifted her gaze from her computer, snapping a smile into place. 'You're in early.'

Declan held out the cake tin he'd brought in. 'Thought we could share this for morning tea for the next hundred years or so,' he said deadpan.

Emma frowned a bit. 'What is it?'

'Fruit cake—old family recipe. Katie sent it via Erinn.'

'That was nice of her.' Emma looked at the rather battered cake tin with its old-fashioned English hunting scene on the lid. 'My Nanna had one of these,' she said with a laugh and got to her feet. 'May I look?'

'Help yourself.'

'Mmm...I love that smell,' Emma inhaled the classic lusciousness of rich dried fruit laced with brandy. 'Pity, though.'

He raised a dark brow.

'I think it'll be long gone before a hundred years are up. I'll leave it in Moira's safekeeping,' she added, replacing the lid carefully. 'Thank Katie when next you speak to her, won't you?'

He nodded absently. There was a beat of silence. Then, softly, as if the words were being pushed up through his diaphragm, 'Are you OK about yesterday, Emma?'

Emma didn't try to misunderstand him. Looking up, she saw the uncertainty clouding his gaze. Lord, she didn't want to have this conversation. She gave a little twist of her shoulder and asked a question of her own, 'How *OK* are you about it?'

Declan felt his heart walk a few flights of stairs. His mouth worked a bit before he answered, 'I'm not.'

'Did you enjoy kissing me, Declan?'

He looked startled at her frankness. Then, throatily, 'I'd have to be dead from the feet up not to have enjoyed kissing you, Emma. You're lovely...'

'Oh!' Suddenly, there was an ache in her stomach that was half pleasure, half pain. And a new awareness was beating its wings all around them.

'We shouldn't let it happen again, though.' Declan sounded as though he was trying to convince himself. His hand reached out towards her cheek, then drew back sharply before it could connect with her skin. 'We're supposed to be operating a professional partnership here, aren't we?'

Her mouth dried. Was he saying they couldn't have both? Yet she ached for him. For the physical closeness they'd found yesterday. For more and more of his long, slow kisses. She was still searching for an acceptable reply when the harsh jangle of the phone in reception split the air.

'Monday morning,' Emma said resignedly.

Within seconds Moira's head popped around the door. 'We have an emergency at the primary school, folks. Neal Drummond needs a doctor there.'

Declan looked a question at Emma. 'Neal's the head teacher,' she said. 'What's happened, Moira?'

'Adam Jones has fallen out of a tree and impaled himself on the fence. It's his upper arm. The child is Carolyn Jones's grandson,' she added for Declan's benefit. 'He's only seven.'

'Then I think we should both go,' Declan said firmly. 'It all sounds a bit iffy.'

'Tsk...' Moira shook her head at the unfairness of it all. 'As if that family needs more trouble.'

'Let's not get bogged down in sentiment, Moira,' Declan growled. 'We can sort all that out later. Let's move it!' He flung the words at Emma from the doorway. 'I'll gather up some gear. Meet you in reception.'

'That's a bit unfeeling.' Moira's feathers were clearly ruffled. 'This could well be the last straw for Carolyn.'

'Declan's still finding his way in rural medicine to some extent,' Emma said diplomatically. 'I imagine the school will have contacted Carolyn but the last thing we need is for her to go into orbit at the accident scene. Whatever else, Adam will have to be kept calm.'

'I'll get her on her mobile then.' Moira as always was one step ahead. 'I'll tell her to go to the school office and wait there. She'll listen to me.'

'Thanks, Moira.' Emma nodded gratefully. 'And prepare her for the fact that Adam will probably have to be sent on to Toowoomba Base. Carolyn will want to go with him.'

'So she'd better pack a bag then.'

'Yes.' Emma picked up her medical case and hurried through to reception.

Declan was already there, taking delivery of the emergency supplies Libby had hastily assembled.

'Paeds drug box, IV kit and emergency oxygen—is that all you need?'

'That's brilliant, Libby, thanks.' Declan slung the emergency pack over his shoulder. He sent a quick grin at the nurse. 'In at the deep end on your first day.'

Libby returned a pert look. 'That's what I'm here for.'

'Not sure how long we'll be,' Emma warned.

'Go!' The RN shooed them towards the outer door. 'Moira and I will juggle the lists around somehow.'

'We'll take my wheels,' Declan said as they sped across the car park. In seconds they were seated and belted up. 'What kind of fence are we talking about here?' He ignited the motor and shot the car towards the street.

'Probably the ten-foot wrought iron fence at the rear of the school grounds,' Emma said. 'There are several huge Moreton Bay figs close to the fence line. I'd guess Adam's scrambled up one of those and fallen.'

'For crying out loud!' Declan muttered, anger and dread in equal portions catching him by surprise. 'Those old spiked fences have no place anywhere near a school!'

'It's precisely because they are *old*,' Emma pointed out patiently. 'They're heritage-listed.'

It was barely half a kilometre to the school but time enough for Emma's uncertainty to intensify at the thought of the possible scenario they were facing.

Neal Drummond was waiting for them. 'Thanks, both of you, for coming,' he said after Emma had made swift introductions.

'What action have you taken so far?' Declan asked quickly.

'Our year one teacher has gone up to Adam. She's physically supporting him as best she can. We've also positioned a couple of ladders so that you'll have access of sorts to the injured child.' Neal escorted them swiftly along to the accident scene.

'So, do you have any idea why Adam went climbing?' Emma asked carefully.

'Don't know yet.' Neal's mouth tightened. 'His grandmother's on her way in. We'll perhaps get a clearer picture then.'

Emma explained what initiative she'd taken to keep Carolyn at arm's length from the accident scene.

'Thanks for that, Emma.' Neal nodded his relief.

'Ambulance, fire and rescue services been alerted?' Declan queried.

'Both ambulances are out on other calls. The base will get one to us asap. Fire and rescue will be here when they can muster a team.' The head teacher ran a hand distractedly over his crew cut. 'We do have a staff member who does regular climbing. He could be of some help in the interim. He's just nipped off home to get his ropes. Right, here we are.'

'Hell's bells!' Declan's face was grim. One look at the accident scene told both doctors it was going to need a painstaking and skilled team effort to achieve a successful outcome for Adam.

Just then, the boy's plaintive little cry, high-pitched and heart-rending, brought the doctors into swift consultation.

'He'll be bordering on shock with the pain.' Emma shaded her eyes, frowning up to where the dense foliage of the tree overhung the fence where the child was impaled. 'That set-up with the ladders isn't going to be effective, Declan. There's no way we can work on Adam like that.'

'Well, not for long,' Declan agreed. 'But if you could manage to get up there and begin the drugs regime...'

'What will you do?' Emma looked worried.

'Wait until the abseiling ropes arrive. Hopefully, I'll be able to secure myself to one of those big branches.' Declan raised his gaze to where the giant fig spread upwards towards the heavens. 'From there I can lower myself almost to the exact spot where Adam is impaled and support him on my lap. That'll allow me the freedom to use both hands to work on him.'

They'd need to intubate. Emma asked hesitantly, 'Sure you're OK with that?' She'd noticed the sudden tautness in Declan's stance. The thinly veiled tension. He was wound tight. Oh, sweet heaven. The uncertainties of his physical fitness must be eating him up. She dived in feet first. 'Do you want to swap roles here?' she asked in a swift aside. 'It's no big deal, if you'd rather…'

'I'm not a cripple, Emma,' Declan shot back with dark impatience. 'Yet!'

'I know—I didn't mean—' Emma swallowed the constriction in her throat, steeling herself as Adam's agonized sobbing almost jettisoned her composure entirely. 'Do what you have to do, then. Just, for heaven's sake, let's get this child some pain relief. Oh—' She turned, catching sight of the male figure sprinting across the quadrangle. 'Here's the bearer of the promised ropes, by the look of it.'

'Mike Foreman,' the young teacher introduced himself. 'What do you want me to do, Doc?'

'We'll need to set up a pulley system.' Declan's response was clipped. The two men went into a huddle.

Emma left them to get on with it. Quashing her fears, she slung the emergency pack over her shoulder and began moving purposefully up the ladder. Her stomach swirled. She breathed deeply and then collected herself. 'Hi.' She looked up shakily to where the young teacher was perched. 'I'm Emma.'

'Chrissy. Are you the doctor?'

'Yes. And you're doing wonderfully, Chrissy.'

'It's been awful, just trying to hold him like this. Poor little boy...'

'I know. Just keep on doing what you're doing. That'll be a great help.' Emma was aware of curtailing her movements, doing everything in slow motion. Adam's broken little sobs spurred her on.

'Hush now, baby,' Emma soothed gently, popping the oxygen mask over the little boy's face. She began assessing her small patient. His skin was cold and clammy, indicating shock. But his pulse and BP were better than she'd feared, raised but stable. Good. She could safely administer the painkiller and anti-nausea drugs. She'd follow up with midazolam. Its light anaesthetic properties would help to combat post-traumatic shock and ease the youngster through the ordeal ahead.

She selected the wide-bore cannula. She was taking no chances with this little one. If Adam began bleeding or, heaven forbid, going into sudden shock, they'd need to run through high-volume fluids to resuscitate him.

But, as long as the foreign object stayed where

it was in Adam's arm, until it could be surgically removed, then the child was reasonably safe from haemorrhaging.

Although they still had a way to go.

With the drugs safely administered, Emma leaned more of her weight into the ladder, using both hands to secure a light absorbent pad around the child's injured arm, and then carefully and gently tucking the youngster into a space blanket. She sent the ghost of a smile to her counterpart.

Chrissy looked on in awe. 'I wouldn't have your job for anything. But, whatever you've given Adam, it's starting to work. I can feel him relaxing.'

'The drugs are doing their job, then. And that sounds like our backup arriving.'

Leaves swirled above them and then Declan's command rang out, 'One more hitch should do it, Mike. Right, I'm here—thanks.' Sitting suspended in his harness, he eased the weight of the child across on to his lap. 'Well done, team.'

Emma felt her heart lift. 'And you,' she rejoined quietly.

'Hmm.' He looked at her narrowly for a moment. 'How's our patient doing?'

'Drifting off.'

'Enough for me to get an airway in?'

'I should think so.'

Declan nodded. 'OK, I'll have a go.'

'I think this is where I leave you, guys.' Chrissy began backing down the ladder.

'The fire and rescue crew are ten minutes away,' Neal Drummond relayed from the foot of the tree.

'Have you got the airway in?' Emma's concern was more immediate.

'Almost there… Right, it's done. With a bit of luck—and heaven knows we've earned it—Adam will be in la-la land by the time the rescue guys get here.'

At last Adam was cut free. At the fireman's signal that the mission had been successful, a subdued cheer went up and, from his anchor in the tree, Mike paid out the guide rope, lowering Declan and his precious cargo to the ground.

'Nice work, folks.' The paramedics had arrived to witness the rescue. 'We'll take over now.' Gently, Adam was stretchered to the waiting vehicle, one officer supporting the little injured arm with the foreign object still *in situ*. 'Heading to Toowoomba Base, right, Emma?'

'Yes, please.' Emma bent over Adam for a final check of the IV line that was running in fluids.

'Just hang on a tick, guys.' Quickly, Declan scribbled some notes to go with their young patient.

'Declan?' Emma said in an urgent undertone.

'I can manage the patient lists if you'd like to go with Adam to the hospital.'

'And what possible use would I be there?' he growled, adding his signature and handing the notes across to the waiting ambulance officer. 'Thanks, mate. We'll be in touch with the surgeon later.'

'No worries, Doc.'

'Adam's grandmother is going with you,' a subdued Emma reminded them.

Jim Yardley, the chief paramedic, raised a hand in acknowledgement. 'All covered, Emma. Thanks.'

There was a strange lull for a few moments after the ambulance had pulled away. A kind of eerie hiatus. Emma heard the soft rustle of leaves above them and looked up. 'I hate this feeling,' she said.

Declan eyed her sharply. 'Adam will be all right, Emma. His arm will be a bit iffy for a while but kids spring back remarkably quickly.'

A furrow etched between her eyes. He just didn't get it. 'I know all that. I just meant the feeling of uncertainty. Wondering why this child did what he did this morning. Was there an upset at home? Should we be taking better care of Carolyn and her needs—the whole family?'

'For crying out loud!' Declan began gathering

up their paraphernalia, impatience in every beat of his movements.

Emma felt her spine stiffen. What kind of response was that? Declan O'Malley had a lot to learn about family medicine, that was for sure. Her teeth bit into the full softness of her lower lip. She didn't need this aggravation. And she didn't need a practice partner who was on a completely different wavelength. After checking they'd left nothing behind, she followed him across to his car.

'Look—' Declan stood awkwardly beside the open lid of the car boot after loading everything inside '—just give me a bit of space here, all right?'

Emma felt a needle of guilt prick her conscience. He sounded on edge and the eyes that lifted to hers were guarded and shadowed. She swallowed. 'Are you OK?'

The corners of his mouth tightened. 'I'm fine.'

Of course he wasn't fine. Her heart bounced sickeningly. She should have realized. He'd spent most of the morning on an emotional roller coaster, no doubt agonizing whether he was going to be able to cut it in a rural practice where physical stamina counted just as much as his medical skills. But he'd done so well. So well. Her gaze faltered. 'Declan—I realize this morning has been difficult so if you feel we need a debrief, you only have to say.'

His blue eyes bored into hers. 'I'll bear it in mind.'

In other words, butt out. *Great.* Emma felt completely put in her place. At this rate they'd be lucky if the contract they'd signed lasted as long as six weeks—let alone six months!

By the time they'd got back to the surgery, Emma knew what she had to do and, by the end of the day, she'd accomplished most of it. She hesitated about telling Declan what she'd done. Would he even care...? Her train of thought was interrupted by the rap on her door and the man himself poked his head in.

'Moira said you'd finished for the day,' he said by way of explanation.

Emma beckoned him in, drawing back in her chair as if to reclaim her space. She took a deep breath, ultra-conscious of him as he walked forward and planted his hands on the desk in front of her. 'What's up?'

'I've an update on Adam. They've operated. Bit of a mess but the foreign object came out cleanly. They'll hit him with antibiotics for the next little while. Should be a straightforward recovery.'

Emma nodded, feeling the awkwardness between

them cloy and magnify. She made a quick decision and swung off her chair. 'Let's go through and get a cup of tea. I'm parched—unless you need to be somewhere else?'

Several expressions chased through his eyes before he said with a rough sigh, 'No... A cuppa sounds good.' He tacked on a forced smile. 'Perhaps we can make some inroads into that fruit cake as well.'

'We'll give it a good shot,' Emma said, relieved that he'd at least agreed to have some down time, if only for a little while.

Switching on the electric jug, she got mugs down from the cupboard, all the time conscious of Declan's restive movements about her kitchen. She cut slabs of the fruit cake and set them on a plate and then, when the water boiled, she made a pot of tea. She didn't care how many cups it took, she was going to make Declan O'Malley talk to her about this morning.

'Delicious cake,' she said a bit later, swiping a crumb from the corner of her mouth. 'Family recipe, you said?'

'Mmm.' Declan was on his second cup of tea. Taking up his mug, he looked at her narrowly over its rim. 'Spit it out, Emma.'

Her eyes widened innocently. 'The cake?'

'No, not the cake.' His voice rumbled with dry

humour. 'You want me to spill my guts about my reactions this morning, don't you?'

Her shoulders twitched. 'I wouldn't have put it quite so bluntly. But if it would help you to talk…'

His blue eyes traced her features one by one, then flicked back to lock with hers, their expression uncertain. 'I—realize I lost it a bit. I jumped all over you. It's the last thing I wanted to do.'

Emma drew in her breath sharply, and suddenly it was there in the air between them. The raw, overwhelming need, the awareness. The fear if it all went wrong. But, for now, they had to stay on track, keep it all professional. She moistened her lips. 'It's OK.'

'It's not OK,' he contradicted. 'I'd like to think it was a one-off but, realistically, I guess I'm going to have to face more of those knife-edge moments in the future—'

'But you'll also learn to cope, Declan,' she responded earnestly.

He snorted. 'Well, let's hope so. Otherwise, I'm not going to be much use to you as a rural doctor, am I?'

'Was it just the fact you doubted your physical capability in the situation?'

'That and the frustration I felt.' He sat back, linking his hands around his mug and staring broodingly into its contents. 'The fact is I *should* have been able to whip Adam into surgery here. Think how much easier it would have been for the family. How much more comfortable for Adam not to have had the road trip to Toowoomba.'

'But it would have been quite the wrong decision for *you*!' Emma's voice was ripe with emotion.

'I know that too,' he agreed, a small rueful twist to his mouth. 'It doesn't make the frustration any less, though.'

'Frustration you can live with,' Emma declared quietly. 'It would be a far worse outcome if you were to rush in when you're not ready.'

'Just to prove a point,' he tacked on dryly.

'Exactly.'

She was wise as well as beautiful. Declan ached to hold her again, feel the silkiness of her hair glide through his fingers. He closed his eyes briefly. He'd better face the fact. Emma Armitage had got to him as no other woman had. Ever. He wanted— *needed* her to think well of him. It mattered. A hell of a lot. He certainly didn't want her to think of him as some kind of lame dog she had to carry in the practice. He blinked and focused as Emma began speaking again.

'Don't keep beating up on yourself over this, Declan. In an ideal situation, the firemen would have been on hand to do the tree climbing today.

We should have had only to carry out our role as doctors. But, like it or not, that's run-of-the-mill rural medicine,' she ended, spreading her hands in a philosophical shrug.

Declan frowned and changed the subject. 'I had a long conversation with Neal Drummond this afternoon.'

'About what?'

'Opening the swimming pool for use by our senior citizens.'

Emma's widened gaze registered her surprise at his proactiveness. 'What was his response?'

'He's willing but he'll have to confer with the school's P&C committee before he can give us an answer. I figured if we could get some water aerobics going for the seniors, it would be of immense benefit health-wise, lessen their stress levels, be a social outlet as well.'

'It would certainly benefit patients like Carolyn Jones. Well done, you.'

Declan's mouth kicked up in a crooked smile. 'Well…I'm slowly getting the hang of this kind of community medicine. Perhaps, by the end of our six months' trial, I'll be taking it in my stride.'

Emma's heart skipped a beat. But if he wasn't— what then? 'Um—I've done a bit of organizing of my own. While Carolyn's away in Toowoomba,

I'm having Adam's two older siblings to stay with me.'

He huffed dryly, 'Why am I not surprised?'

'I'm a hands-on kind of girl,' she defended.

'I'd have to agree with that.' The look he sent her was blue-metal hot.

Emma's insides heaved crazily. She felt heat rising, warming her throat, flowering over her cheeks. Suddenly, her train of thought was gone, her thoughts all over the place. 'It just seemed the logical thing to do.' The words pumped up jerkily from her chest. 'Lauren and Joel know me. Before their lives went pear-shaped, Carolyn did some housekeeping for Dad and me. The kids used to come with her sometimes. They had the run of the house. Moira's round there now, helping them pack a few clothes. The school bus can pick them up from here in the mornings and drop them back. It'll be good.'

Declan's gaze softened. 'You're so like your father, Emma. He believed in actions speaking louder than words too.'

Emma dipped her head, sudden tears blurring her eyes. He couldn't have given her a nicer compliment.

CHAPTER SIX

CHILDREN made the house a home, Emma thought indulgently, watching as Lauren and Joel scooped up their breakfast cereal with obvious enjoyment. 'Now, I'll get on and make your school lunches,' she said, placing some buttered toast on the table between them. 'What would you like on your sandwiches, guys?'

'Anything will do,' ten-year-old Lauren said shyly.

Blue-eyed Joel sent an innocent look at Emma. 'It's tuck shop today.'

'We're not allowed tuck shop.' Lauren gave her younger brother an old-fashioned look.

Probably because their grandparents couldn't afford to hand out money they didn't have. Emma's soft heart was touched. Poor babes. 'Why don't we have a treat today, then? Let's do tuck shop.'

The children stopped eating and looked at Emma. 'Could we?' Lauren fisted a small hand across her chest.

'You bet,' Emma said.

'Yay!' Joel yelped with delight. 'Can I have a burger?'

'Please,' Emma directed, hiding a smile.

'Please...' Joel parroted with a grin.

'What about you, Lauren?' Emma sent the little girl a warm smile. 'Like a burger as well?'

Lauren nodded her wheat-blonde head. 'Yes, please, Emma.'

'Good. Now, what do we have to do—write out an order or something?' Emma racked her brains thinking back to her own primary school days.

'We write what we want on a piece of paper and put it in our lunch box with the money.' Joel was only too happy to provide the answers.

'And the tuck shop ladies make up the lunch orders,' Lauren filled in quietly.

'Right.' Emma looked from one to the other. 'That sounds easy-peasy.'

Lauren giggled.

'And you can get other stuff too,' Joel said around a mouthful of toast.

Emma reached for her scribble pad and a pen. 'Let's get started, then.' While the two pairs of young eyes watched intently, she wrote the orders for the burgers and then asked, 'Now, what else would you like, Lauren?'

The little girl thought for a minute. 'Could I have a strawberry yoghurt, please?'

'Of course, you may.' Emma wrote diligently. 'Joel, honey?'

'Packet of chips—please?'

Emma raised a brow. It wasn't the most nutritious of choices, but hey, today's lunches were meant to be a treat. 'OK, done.' Emma stuffed the notes into the waiting lunch boxes and enclosed the appropriate money. 'Now, if you've finished breakfast, hop off and brush your teeth.'

Joel took off along the hallway, making *vroom* noises as he flapped his arms like an aeroplane coming in to land, almost colliding with Declan, who was making his way in. 'What's that all about?' Declan cranked a dark brow in query.

Emma chuckled. 'Joel's on a high because I said they could have tuck shop today.

'He's not the only one on a high.' Declan's eyes and voice teased.

'It's lovely having them here.' Emma's blood sang. 'This house was made for children.'

And perhaps she'd fill it with her own one day. The wild idea of him being the father of those imaginary children stopped Declan in his tracks, sending rivers of want and doubt and sheer amazement cascading through his bloodstream. The thought was crazy… 'Er…I came in early. Thought you might want a bit of a hand. But I see I needn't have worried.'

'No—' She saw his gaze settle on her mouth and linger. And suddenly she could feel his presence, his masculinity like the ticking of a time bomb... 'They're great kids. Ah—here they are again. All set?' She snuggled them into their anoraks, gave Lauren a hug and laughed as Joel squirmed away. Handing them their backpacks, she ushered them outside to wait for the school bus.

'It's cold out there—' Emma was rubbing her arms as she came back into the warmth of the kitchen. 'Would you like a cup of tea?'

'I've put the kettle on for a fresh pot.'

'Oh—good. That's good.' Emma's voice trailed away and she glanced at her watch. 'You *are* in early.

'I couldn't stay away. It's more fun here.'

There was a moment of awkward silence while they smiled at each other in a goofy kind of way. Then the water boiled and Declan turned away to make the tea. Tea made, he turned back with the pot cradled in his hands. 'Am I making myself too much at home here? Just yell if I am.'

'No—it's nice...' The words spilled out on their own and she squirmed at her transparent honesty. 'I'll get the mugs.'

'So—did you happen to find out the reasons for Adam's misadventure?' Declan asked her.

'Mmm, I did, actually. I had a little chat to

Lauren last night when she was getting ready for bed. I didn't press her,' she added, seeing Declan's sharp look of concern. 'Lauren volunteered the information. She said her gran lost her temper and smacked Adam on the legs.'

Declan's mouth drew in. 'Hard?'

'With a rolled-up newspaper.'

So, not too hard, then. They didn't need a case of child abuse to add to the already difficult situation. 'What was the problem?'

'Adam wet the bed—again.'

'He's obviously disturbed. Poor little kid.' Declan shook his head. 'So, as doctors, what do we do—start looking for definitive solutions for this family?'

'If there are any.' Emma sighed. 'Carolyn will be beside herself.'

'Wallowing in guilt is not going to solve anything.'

'That's a bit hard.'

'So is what's happening to these kids. Be realistic, Emma. Do we know where the mother is?'

'Tracey?' Emma pulled her thoughts together. 'Toowoomba somewhere, I think. Carolyn has an address.'

'So, will she let Tracey know what's happened?'

'I don't think they speak much.'

Declan blew out a frustrated breath through his

teeth. 'So, Tracey is living in a twilight zone with her junkie boyfriend while the grandparents slave their guts out to raise *her* kids. That's not good enough. Those kids need their mother.'

'They need a functioning mother,' Emma countered. 'And stability—which they have now with their grandparents.'

'They could still have that but Tracey should be there as well, sharing the load. Carolyn and Nev are nearing an age when they should be thinking of enjoying their retirement. They shouldn't have this extra burden of having to rear their grandchildren because their daughter-in-law chooses to opt out of her responsibilities.'

Emma rolled her eyes. 'So, what are you going to do—drag Tracey back by the hair and make her be a proper mother to her kids?'

'No, Dr Armitage.' Surprisingly, Declan grinned. 'I'll go and see her, talk to her and try to get her into some decent rehab programme.'

'You're quite serious about this, aren't you?'

'Yes, I am.' Declan's look turned pensive. 'I'm remembering my own childhood, when our lives suddenly turned upside-down.'

'I don't see the connection,' Emma said. '*Your* mother appears to have made a wonderful job of raising you and your sisters.'

He shrugged. 'Given a different set of genes,

who knows how she might have coped? It's both as simple and as complicated as that. Anyway, I'd like to try to see Tracey. Ascertain what I can do to help.'

Emma was about to offer to accompany him but she held back. She guessed this was something he needed to do off his own bat. He was on a steep learning curve but he seemed to be getting the hang of family medicine with all its uncertainties and pitfalls. She should be grateful. 'When will you go?' she asked instead.

'This afternoon, if I can get away reasonably early. I'll make a few phone calls first, see what's out there in the way of help for Tracey. When I get to Toowoomba, I'll swing by the hospital and see Adam, have a word with Carolyn and hope she can give me Tracey's address.'

'Just—don't expect too much, Declan, from yourself or—' Emma's flow of words was interrupted by a loud banging on the front door of the surgery. She jumped to her feet.

'Wait!' Declan cautioned. 'Let me get the door.'

Emma stopped mid-stride. 'But surely it's an emergency!'

'We don't know that for sure. And people are aware you live alone, Emma.'

'Oh—' Beating back a shadowy unease, Emma

fell in behind Declan as he went to the front door. Switching off the alarm, he unlocked the door and slid it open. 'Yes?'

A man dressed in workman's clothes rocked agitatedly from one foot to the other. At Declan's appearance, he pulled back uncertainly. 'You a doctor, mate?'

'Yes, I am.' Declan's response was clipped. 'What's happened?'

The man jerked a thumb over his shoulder. 'I'm the foreman from the building site across the road, there. One of the guys slipped off the scaffolding—tore his hand on a bloody wall spike. Bleeding's pretty bad.'

'You go!' Emma practically pushed Declan out of the door. 'I'll follow with my bag.'

As quickly as she could, Emma followed the men across the road to the site. 'Who and what do we have here?' She hunkered down beside Declan.

'Brett Cartrell, de-gloved hand.' Declan's dark head was bent over his patient. 'Did you bring morphine?'

Emma delved into her case and handed him the drug plus an anti-nausea medication. Ah... not good. She clamped her teeth on her bottom lip, seeing where the skin had been forcibly pulled back from the workman's hand. The injury would surely need microsurgery.

'Crikey, Doc...' Brett was pale and sweating. 'This is killin' me—'

'I know, mate.' Declan slipped the oxygen mask into place. 'Breathe away, now. That's good. IV now, please, Emma.' He shot the painkiller home. 'Normal saline.'

Emma knew it was their best option to stave off shock. Prompting a vein to the surface, she slid the cannula into place.

'What's the ETA on the ambulance?' Declan brought his gaze up, addressing the shocked faces of the men around him.

'They'll be a while, the base reckoned,' Cam Creedy, the foreman, said.

'God, I love that euphemistic term,' Declan growled, running a stethoscope over Brett's chest. 'Breathing's OK,' he relayed in an aside to Emma. 'Could you get a pressure bandage over the injury, please?'

Quickly and gently, Emma secured the bandage. 'Sling now?'

Declan nodded. 'I'll hold his hand steady while you do that.' He addressed the site foreman. 'I take it you'll be doing a report for the Workplace Health and Safety people?'

'Goes without saying.' Cam Creedy pushed

back his hard hat and scratched his head. 'I don't know how it could have happened. I always get the guys to check and double-check before they climb anywhere.'

'Accidents happen,' Declan said darkly. 'I can vouch for that.'

Emma sent him a sharp look. He seemed in control and there was none of the edginess of yesterday. She daren't ask him if he was OK. He'd probably shoot her down in flames and she didn't want that. Not when they seemed to be forging a more positive kind of relationship.

'Here's the ambulance,' someone said.

After the handover, they walked back across the road to the surgery. 'So, when can we expect the third?' Declan asked.

'Sorry?'

'Accidents usually happen in threes, don't they?'

'Who said that?' Emma looked at him with scepticism.

'No one of note, but haven't you noticed when, for instance, your car packs up, then something else breaks down and then you wait with trepidation for the third thing to go wrong?'

'That's rubbish!'

'That's what the guy said when he accidentally threw out an antique vase worth thousands.'

'You're making it up.'

'We'll see,' he grinned, standing aside for her to precede him through the front door of the surgery. 'Morning all.'

Jodi avidly sought details of what had occurred. And then shrieked, 'Yeuch! Declan—look at your shirt! It's all bloody.'

'That's the third one,' Declan deadpanned, holding the offending garment away from his chest. He turned to Emma. 'My shirt's ruined. See, told you so.'

'You fool.' Emma's chuckle was rich and warm. 'Come through and I'll find you a spare one.'

Later that afternoon, Declan made his way to the address Carolyn had given him—reluctantly. 'Tracey won't come back,' the grandmother had said as they'd sat over a cup of coffee in the annexe off the children's ward.

'Have you told her about Adam's accident?' Declan had asked gently.

'She wouldn't be interested. Nev and I will have to rear these children as best we can.' Her shoulders lifted in a weary sigh and the corners of her mouth wilted unhappily. 'Ryan wouldn't have wanted this for us.'

'I don't imagine he'd have wanted this for Tracey

either,' Declan pointed out with quiet diplomacy. 'Was he your only son?'

'Our only child. We couldn't have any more.' She paused. 'And I suppose I could have tried harder with Tracey…' Carolyn's mouth trembled. 'She's only a little thing. The babies took it out of her… her own mother was useless, no help there.'

Now, Declan hesitated before gingerly ascending the shallow steps. What a falling-down dump. The verandah was crumbling and sagging on rotten footings and saplings and long-stemmed weeds were shoving up through the cracks in the floor-boards. He stood on the edge of the verandah and looked out, feeling a surge of anger swell in his chest. This just wasn't on…

'Whaddya want?'

Declan turned, his jaw tightening.

A young man was standing at the front door. He looked malnourished and unkempt, his hair dreadlocked and grubby, his skin pasty. 'You a cop?'

'No,' Declan said clearly. 'I'm a doctor.'

'We didn't send for no doctor. You're narc squad, ain't yer? Leave us alone…'

'Sorry, can't manage that.' Declan took a step forward. 'I need to see Tracey.'

'You can't—just—just leave us alone…' the young man whined, trying to block Declan's entry, but his slight build was no match for Declan's powerful bulk. 'Hey—you hurt me!' he yelped accusingly, trying to regain his balance. 'I'll get ya for this—'

'Whatever works,' Declan said through clenched teeth. A few strides took him to the end of the short hallway leading to an enclosed back verandah-cum-kitchen. There was a sight that had his worst fears realized. Tracey Jones looked a washed-out, defeated figure.

She was standing against a set of louvred windows, the light from the solitary naked bulb elongating her shadow. She was barefoot and wearing a threadbare dressing gown. Her stance spoke of defiance mixed with a fear so tangible Declan felt he could almost reach out and touch it. 'Hello, Tracey,' he said gently. 'I'm Declan O'Malley, your children's doctor from the Kingsholme practice. I've come to tell you Adam's had an accident. He's in hospital.'

Tracey gave an audible gasp and her hand flew to her mouth. 'It's not my fault—' She shrank back as if she'd been threatened with violence.

'No one is saying it is, Tracey. But you're Adam's mother and we need to talk about that.'

There was a long silence. Then Tracey slowly moved forward as if sleep-walking and sank down on one of the old wooden chairs set against the rickety kitchen table. She bowed her head and clasped her hands between her knees. 'My kids must hate me…'

Declan let the statement go unanswered. Instead, he cast a quick all-encompassing look around him. It was a scene of abject poverty. He'd expected no less but he'd also expected chaos and there he'd been wrong. Every surface was scrubbed clean; even the mismatched crockery was washed and stacked neatly on the shabby dresser. Declan's jaw worked for a second. It was a pathetic sight, yet he sensed hope that something could be salvaged here.

He pulled out a chair and sat down with Tracey at the table, his hands placed squarely in front of him. 'Would you like to see your children again, Tracey?'

'They wouldn't want to see me,' the young woman whispered brokenly. 'I—left them.'

'Mind telling me why you did that?' Declan's voice carried a gentle reassurance.

There was a long silence while Tracey rubbed at a spot on the edge of the table.

'I guess you were gutted when Ryan was killed,' Declan surmised. 'Maybe you flipped out, lost the plot for a while. Am I right?'

Tracey's gaze sprang to his. 'Yes…' she said on a ragged breath. 'H-how did you know?'

'I've been there.' Declan's voice flattened. 'Life gets complicated. Sometimes it's hard to ask for help, even when we know we should. I can give you that help now, Tracey, if you want it badly enough.'

Tracey made a sound somewhere between a sob and a moan. She looked at Declan, the pain of loss and uncertainty in her eyes.

'Your kids miss you…' Declan's smile warmed the bleak little kitchen. 'They need you. And I think you need them. If I didn't think that, I wouldn't be here.'

'Where are they now?' Tracey's gaze widened in query, her question a whispered plea. 'And what happened to my baby?'

Quietly and non-judgementally, Declan filled her in.

'I don't suppose Carolyn will ever forgive me,' Tracey said bitterly. 'She never wanted Ryan to marry me but I was pregnant with Lauren and we loved each other, despite what she said. But I had the kids so quickly and Ryan was away a lot. It was hard…'

'I know. Carolyn knows that too now. I think she and Nev would be over the moon if you came back.'

Tracey pressed a lock of hair to her cheek, her eyes wide with fear and doubt. 'I couldn't just rock back as if—as if nothing has happened. I'd need someone to help me.' She sent Declan a beseeching look. 'Could you... Dr O'Malley?'

Declan nodded, as if her response was what he'd hoped for. 'I can do that, Tracey.' He paused and then, 'When was your last fix?'

Tracey drew back sharply, her expression shocked. 'I never injected! I only took a few pills and that—not enough to get hooked on anything. It was just something to...make the pain go away. And Robbie kept getting them for me.' Her teeth came down on her bottom lip. 'He's garbage. I never want to see him again.'

'I don't think you need worry about *him*. I'd say he's done a runner. Now—' Declan pushed his chair back and stood to his feet '—let's get you sorted, Tracey Jones. What do you say?'

Tracey scrambled awkwardly to her feet. 'I'd like a shower but there's no hot water.'

'Do you have clothes?'

'Some—the ones I brought with me. And they're clean,' she added with an edge of defiance.

'Go and get dressed, then,' Declan said kindly. 'And pack up what you want to take with you.'

'Everything?' It was a frightened whisper.

Declan's look was implacable. 'You won't be coming back, Tracey.'

Her throat jerked as she swallowed. 'Then what?'

'You'll come with me to the women's shelter. You can have a shower and a hot meal and they'll give you a bed. I'll leave you a mild sleeper so you'll get some decent rest.'

'How...long can I stay there?'

'As long as you need. No one is about to judge you, Tracey, please believe that. The people at the shelter will arrange a medical check-up for you and, later on, some counselling, if that's what you'd like.'

'OK...' Tracey nodded. 'I s'pose I could talk to someone.'

'Good.' Declan smiled again. 'I'll check in with the shelter each day and, as soon as you're feeling up to it, I'll take you to see Adam.'

About a kilometre out of Bendemere, Declan pressed Emma's logged-in number on his hands-free phone. She answered on the third ring. 'Where are you?'

'Nearly home.'

'How did it go with Tracey?'

'OK, I think. Long story. Could I swing by?'

'Of course. Have you eaten?'

'No. Have you?'

'Not yet.'

'I'll pick up some takeaway, then.'

'No need.' There was a hint of laughter in her voice as she added, 'I've made a curry.'

'It must be your destiny to feed me,' he responded, matching her jokey tone.

'Mmm. Must be.'

'Are the kids OK?'

'They're fine. I've just tucked them in. Lauren's reading *The Wind in the Willows*.'

'Ah—I loved those guys—especially old Badger. Who's Lauren's favourite?'

'Moley, I think. She says he's cuddly.'

'Nice.' Declan laughed lightly. Oh, boy. He began to feel almost punch-drunk. The tone of the conversation was doing strange things to his insides. It could have been *their* kids they were talking about. An unfulfilled yearning as sudden as a lightning strike filled his veins.

Emma.

Who else in the whole of his adult life had ever made him feel this way? As though his feet were hardly touching the ground, his head in the stars.

But at the same time scared him to blazes...

What was happening here? Emma began to set the table, a mixture of a kind of thrilling uncertainty and just plain happiness flooding her. *Declan.* Her practice partner. Her friend. Yes, he was both of those. But he had become more than that. Unless she was reading it all wrong.

But she didn't think so. Lately, he'd been watching her in that way he had. Kind of thoughtful and expectant all mixed up together. And a little bemused, as though he didn't quite know what universe he'd stumbled into. Let alone why he had.

And there was more. Emma pressed her fingers to her mouth, reliving his kisses all over again. Parting her lips, she imagined tasting him again, just the action flooding her body with sensation and desire...

'Emma?'

'Ooh!' she squealed and spun round from her X-rated reverie to see him hovering at the kitchen door. Her hand flew to her throat. 'I didn't hear you arrive,' she said, all flustered.

'I was quiet,' he said, moving inside. 'Didn't want to wake the kids.'

'I've just checked on them. They're well away.' She went towards him and they met in the middle of the kitchen. 'What do you have there?' Emma indicated the carrier bag he was toting.

'Some wine and a chocolate dessert.'

'Lovely. But you didn't need to—' Emma felt she could hardly breathe.

'I can't keep letting you feed me.'
Oh, you can, you can.

Emma savoured the last of her dessert as it rolled off her tongue. 'Oh, that was gorgeous,' she said with a sigh.

'Not bad,' Declan said. 'I think the packaging might have been a bit deceptive all the same.' In fact the dessert had turned out to be nothing more exotic than a rich vanilla ice cream with a swirl of chocolate and a sprinkling of hazelnuts. 'No doubt the kids will finish it off.'

'Mmm, they'll love it. Coffee?'

'No, thanks.' Declan rolled his shoulders and stretched. 'Do you have a green tea, by any chance?'

'I have a whole selection of organic teas,' Emma said grandly, getting lightly to her feet. 'I'll have a peppermint, I think.' She made the tea quickly, passed a mug to Declan and then resumed her chair. 'Are you going to fill me in about your visit to Tracey now?'

Declan did, quickly and concisely.

Emma looked thoughtful. 'You don't think she'll do a runner from the shelter, do you?'

Declan took a mouthful of his tea. 'No...' he said eventually. 'Her self-esteem has taken a battering. But, unless I'm a very poor judge of character, I think she'll be back with her kids quite soon. She's had a huge wake-up call. And Carolyn's anxious to mend fences as well. I'm tipping they'll forge a workable relationship when things settle down.'

'Should we say anything to Lauren and Joel yet?'

'Not yet. I have faith in Tracey but I'd hate to raise the kids' hopes and see them dashed. Let's tread carefully for the next little while.'

'You're right.' She gave a short nod. And then the emotions from a very crowded couple of days kicked in and she said without thinking, 'You've no idea how wonderful it is to have someone to talk to about this stuff. And not even on a professional level—just to talk to.'

'Oh, but I do, Emma,' he said softly. 'I couldn't wait to get back and talk to *you*.'

She blinked. He was watching her in *that* way again. 'I guess it's good, then—that we can communicate so well. For the success of the practice,' she concluded, the words so far from where her thoughts had travelled, they made no sense at all.

'Why are you spinning this, Emma?' Declan kept his voice low. 'What's happening here is about us—you and me. We could have met anywhere in the world but we just happened to meet here. The practice has nothing to do with it.'

'I'm afraid...' she heard herself say.

'Of me?' His voice rose. 'Or of what we could mean to each other?'

'You were all for cooling things between us very recently,' she accused bluntly.

'Yeah—well, I was nuts to think emotions could be put in little boxes and only opened when it seemed the right time. There's no *right time*. Is there?'

Emma's green eyes flew wide with indecision.

'Don't you trust me?' His tone was still patient.

She licked her lips. 'I once trusted a man with my whole life...'

'I know about that.' Declan's gaze didn't waver.

'Dad told you?' Emma fisted a hand against her breast. 'He *told* you?'

'Normally, he wouldn't have broken your confidence. You must know that. But he was worn down, worried about the future—your future. And, whoever he was, the man who let you go was an idiot.'

'So you're implying I fell in love with an idiot?'

'He might have been a charming idiot,' Declan compromised. 'They exist.'

'He was sleeping with my best friend.' With the benefit of time blurring the pain, Emma found she could talk about it objectively. 'It was going on right under my nose and I didn't twig. And when Marcus finally had the decency to tell me he wanted to break our engagement, *she* had the gall to suggest there was no reason why we couldn't still be friends!'

'I hope you got mad.'

'Mad enough.' Emma smiled unwillingly. 'When I finally steeled myself to go round to our apartment to collect the rest of my things, Marcus was there.'

'And?' Declan's mouth twitched.

'He was embarrassed as hell. Said he was just nipping out to the shops. In other words, he hoped I'd be gone by the time he got back.'

'Bad move.' Declan's eyes glinted wickedly. 'And you *were* gone, of course.'

'Of course.' Emma sliced him a grin. 'But not before I'd interrupted the wash cycle he'd left going and chucked in a pair of my red knickers with all his obscenely expensive white business shirts.'

'Wow!' Declan looked impressed. 'I see I'll have to watch my back around you, Dr Armitage.'

She made a face at him and then, 'I was in a well of self-pity for a long time. That's probably why I didn't notice Dad's deteriorating health.'

'But you're over this guy, Marcus, now?'

'The man was indeed an idiot,' she said with asperity.

'So, we agree on something at last. Come on.' Declan reached for her hand across the table. 'Walk me out. It's time I went home.' There was regret in his voice and his eyes had gone dark.

'You could stay here tonight.'

There was a beat of silence.

A thousand questions wanted to leap off Declan's tongue. But he held back. Obviously, she hadn't meant stay as in *stay*. And, even if she had, it was too soon.

For both of them.

'There are a zillion bedrooms in this place,' Emma explained jerkily—just in case he'd imagined...

'There would be. It's a big house.'

'Um—thank you for today and everything. I have a feeling it will all turn out—'

'Stop.' He pressed his finger against her lips. 'This is about us, Emma.'

'Is it?' Her hands went to his waist. 'Shame we don't seem to have come up with any solutions *about us.*'

'On the contrary.' His voice dropped to a husky undertone. 'I think we've lit a bit of a lamp tonight, don't you?'

A lamp to find their way? Could it be as simple

as that? Emma closed her eyes, giving herself up to the pure sensation of his hands running over her back, whispering against the soft cotton of her shirt.

'Come on the journey with me...' Declan bent to kiss her, tenderly at first, as if to soothe away her doubts and fears, then with an eagerness and urgency, as if to imprint his faith on what they had together.

Was this the time to let her feelings run free and just *trust* him? Emma agonized as she opened her mouth under his and kissed him back.

CHAPTER SEVEN

IT WAS two days later and Lauren was icing cup cakes with Emma at the kitchen table after school. 'Is Mum ever coming home?'

Oh, please heaven, *yes*, Emma thought, her eyes clouding, but what to tell this sweet child? 'Lauren,' she said carefully, leaning over and gently curving her hand around Lauren's slender little wrist. 'Your Mum's been sick.'

'Like vomiting and stuff?' Lauren asked.

'Well, not quite like that. But a lot of worries have made her sad and just not able to be with you all.'

Lauren set two huge dark eyes on Emma. 'How do you mean?'

Emma's mind scrabbled for a truth that might be acceptable. And then in a flash she remembered the explanation one of her trainers in paeds had given to a child whose circumstances had not been dissimilar to Lauren's.

'You've seen a balloon burst, haven't you, Lauren?'

The little girl's eyes widened and then she nodded.

'Well, your mum's problems just kept piling up and up and each problem was like another puff into the balloon. And then it was just one problem too many and the balloon exploded.'

'And she ran away...'

'Yes.' Emma met the child's gaze steadily.

Lauren looked suddenly lost. 'Was she mad at us?'

'Oh, honey, no...' Emma scooped the little girl close to her. 'Your mum was just mixed up.' Emma smoothed a hand over Lauren's fair hair. 'But she's been staying with some people who are helping her and she's feeling so much better, we think she'll be home with you again before too long.' Emma mentally crossed her fingers about that. But, from what Declan had said only that morning, it seemed Tracey had made a remarkable turn-around and had begun a tentative reconnection with Carolyn. Tomorrow, Declan was taking her to see Adam at the hospital.

'She might be back in time for our sports day,' Lauren said, her little hand still trustingly in Emma's.

'Yes, she just might.' Oh, Tracey, please don't

screw up, Emma pleaded silently to the absent mum. Please come home where you belong.

The next morning, Emma welcomed a new patient, Rina Kennedy, into her consulting room. 'You're new to our community?'

'We've just bought the garden centre,' Rina answered in her soft Irish brogue.

'That's interesting,' Emma said. 'It looked like closing there for a while.'

Rina made a face. 'I don't think the former owners had a clue what they were doing. But we aim to fix all that. It'll be grand when we've done a makeover.'

'Very good luck with it, then.' Emma smiled. 'Now, Mrs Kennedy, what can I do for you today?'

'Call me Rina for starters. And I hope you don't think I've gone soft in the head for coming to see you, Doctor, but I wanted to ask you about the best way to avoid getting sun damage to our skin. We've been hearing such terrible things about skin cancer since we've moved to Australia and our two little girls have the fairest complexions.'

'You're right to be concerned,' Emma said. 'Our summers here are hotter and the sun's rays far more intense than you'd be used to in the Northern hemisphere.'

'That's what I thought...'

'But mostly,' Emma went on, 'folk who suffer sun damage to their skin can only blame themselves, because they don't take a blind bit of notice of what health professionals have been telling them for years. And that is to stay out of the sun in the hottest part of the day, to cover up with light protective clothing and, most importantly, to use sunscreen with the highest protection factor. A thirty-plus rating is the best.'

'Could you write all that down for me, please, Doctor?'

Emma smiled. 'I'll give you some fact sheets and you can read up on it. But if you're sensible and keep a healthy respect for what excessive exposure to the sun can do, you shouldn't have any problems.'

Rina jerked a hand at the window. 'It's a lovely garden you have out there,' she said with an impish grin. 'But there's always room for another shrub or two,' she added, unashamedly drumming up business. 'You must come along to our official opening when we've done our revamp. We'll have some grand bargains.'

Emma's head went back as she laughed. 'Let's know the date and I'll make sure all our folk from the practice are there with bells on and nice fat wallets,' she promised. What a nice cheery person, she thought. Spirits lighter, Emma began to make her way through the day's patient list and, at the end of it, she popped in on Declan.

'Hi.' He looked up from his computer, his eyes crinkling into a smile.

'Is our Friday staff meeting still on?''

'Hell, yeah. This is where we function properly as a practice. Thrash out all the hairy bits.'

Watching his strong mouth, so sexy in repose, curve upwards in a smile, Emma felt her heart pick up speed. 'See you shortly, then.'

'I can't believe how the time seems to be flying these days.' Moira looked around the team with a happy smile. 'Mind you, they say it does when you're having fun.'

'It's certainly been interesting,' Declan said. 'OK, folks, any problems?'

'Cedric Dutton,' Libby said with feeling. 'One of our patients on the list for a home visit.'

Declan reclined in his chair and stretched out his legs. 'What's up with Mr Dutton?'

'For starters, he lives alone. He had a stroke some while ago. He was treated in Toowoomba Base. But he's not reclaiming his independence at all.'

'Do we know why not?' Declan cut to the chase.

Libby shook her head. 'The Rotary arranged the

necessary safety modifications to his house, and the meals on wheels folk call but he appears to be just sitting in front of the television. It's not like he doesn't know better—he's an educated man. He used to work as a surveyor with the council.'

Declan's eyes lit with sympathy. 'The stroke will have come as a great shock to him.'

'If Mr Dutton's not moving about, we have to be concerned about pressure sores.' Emma looked keenly at Libby.

'We do,' Libby agreed. 'And he's so very thin. But he wouldn't let me touch him, let alone explain anything. There are a dozen things he could be doing to gain a much better quality of life.'

Declan's mouth drew in. 'Possibly there's a residue of post-trauma. Sounds like he's scared to try himself out. Does he have family?'

'He's a bachelor,' Libby said. 'Extended family in Brisbane.'

'Has anyone talked to him about the stroke itself?' Declan queried. 'The repercussions to his body?'

'I imagine the nurses tried but he's such an old chauvinist,' Libby emphasized with a roll of her eyes. 'He called me *girlie!*'

Declan cracked a laugh. 'Want me to have a word, then, Libs?'

'Please, Declan, if you have time. He lives in

one of the cottages along by the old railway line, number fourteen. Seems very much a loner, from what I could gather.'

'Possibly another candidate for our water walking if we can get it up and running,' Declan considered. 'Which reminds me, I've been invited to a meeting of the school's P&C committee on Monday night. It's on the agenda to be discussed.'

'Hey, that's great,' Libby enthused. 'I've a list a mile long of folk who'd benefit. We'd possibly need to arrange transport, though.'

'The council could be pressed into doing that,' Moira contributed.

'Hang on, people.' Declan lifted a staying hand. 'We've only got to first base yet.'

'But it's a positive first step and all down to you,' Emma said, enthusiastic and proud on his behalf.

Declan acknowledged Emma's praise with a twist of his hand. Rocking forward, he doodled something on his pad and thought life played weird tricks sometimes. *Very weird.* A year ago, he'd never in his wildest dreams have imagined he'd be here in rural Queensland practicing family medicine. Rather, he'd expected to be planning a quick rise to the top in his chosen field in one of Australia's big teaching hospitals…

Emma was now so tuned in to his body language she could read Declan like a book. He was doing his best to settle in, even enjoying the challenge to some extent. But was he also acknowledging that community medicine could never match the heart-pumping discipline of being a top-flight surgeon? And, if he was, could he let his dreams go so easily? Suddenly, the six months he'd promised for their trial period seemed so little time to work out whether they had a future together.

Or apart.

'Oh, Emma, while I think of it—' Moira cast a quick enquiring look across the table '—Jodi wondered whether Lauren and Joel would like to spend some time out at the stables tomorrow. Apparently, there are a couple of quiet ponies they could ride and Jodi would be there to supervise them. She thought—well, we both thought—it might be a nice treat for them and, being Saturday, it could help fill in the time a little?'

Emma was touched by Moira and Jodi's kindness. In truth, she'd been wondering how she could keep the kids occupied over a whole weekend. There wasn't a lot to do in Bendemere. She jumped at the offer. 'I'm sure they'd love it, Moira. But is Jodi sure it's OK with the McGintys?'

Moira shrugged. 'My granddaughter could sweet-talk a crow into singing like a canary if she had a mind to. I'll tell her it's all right then, shall I?'

Emma nodded. 'Did she mention a time?'

'Morning's good. And, speaking of the children—' Moira looked at her watch. 'Do you need to see to them?'

'No, they're spending the night back home with their grandfather.' Emma smiled. 'He was picking them up from school. Promised them pizza for tea, I believe.'

'Good old Nev,' Moira nodded in approval. 'How's Tracey doing?' she asked gently. The whole practice in one way or another was now involved in the Jones's ongoing saga and were all rooting for the family to be healed and reunited.

Declan rubbed a hand across his chin. 'I'm visiting Tracey tomorrow. She thinks she's ready to see Adam. I'm picking up Nev and taking him along with me. He, at least, seems very optimistic things will work out.'

'He's the calming influence on Carolyn,' Moira said wisely. 'And he's always had a soft spot for Tracey.'

'There's still a fair bit of sorting out to do yet.' Declan was cautious. 'Now, anything else on the agenda, guys?'

There wasn't a lot, so the meeting wrapped up quickly and Libby and Moira left.

'How optimistic are you, really, about Tracey getting things together?' Emma looked earnestly at Declan, her chin resting in her upturned hand.

'Reasonably.' He flexed a hand. 'I've spoken to her on the phone each night and she's surprised me with her turnaround. But then, the folk at the shelter have been working with her and her self-esteem has received a huge boost. Apparently, she's been absorbing the counselling sessions like a sponge.'

'Lauren has been quietly eating her little heart out about things, worrying whether her mum left because she was mad at them. I tried to reassure her and I hope I haven't jumped the gun but I indicated Tracey might be back home soon.'

'It's best to keep positive around the kids,' Declan said slowly. 'I mean, what's the alternative?'

Emma bit her lip. 'Awful,' she agreed.

'Hey, don't let's drop the ball.' In an abrupt gesture of reassurance, Declan pressed her hand and then got to his feet. 'Are you busy tonight?'

'Er...no.'

'Like to go out somewhere to eat later?'

'Um...' Emma flannelled. He'd taken her by surprise. 'Where would we go?'

'You choose. Better phone and book, though. It's Friday night.'

'OK… Are you heading home now?' she asked as they walked slowly along the hallway and through to the main part of the house and eventually to the kitchen.

'I thought I'd call in on Libby's old chap first. See what I can sort out for him. I'll pick you up about seven?'

'Or we could meet at the restaurant.'

'Let's be old-fashioned.' His mouth tipped at the corner. 'I'll call for you.'

Emma pulled back, her nerve ends pinching alarmingly. So, were they going on a date? The thought thrilled her and panicked her in equal measure. 'Fine. Seven's good.'

As Declan opened the back door, a gale-force wind nearly knocked him back inside. 'Hell's bells, when did the weather turn foul like this?'

'Ages ago, probably without our knowing. We've been cloistered indoors. And it's freezing, Declan.'

'Rats!' Declan turned up the collar on his windcheater. 'After Scotland, this is nothing.'

Emma began to rub her upper arms vigorously. 'You won't say that when the power lines come down.'

'Is that likely?'

'It's happened a few times since I've been here.'

'Snap decision then.' His eyes narrowed on

her face and suddenly the intensity of his regard hardened, as though he'd made up his mind about something. 'Change of plan. I'll drop by Cedric's, then head home for a shower and, on my way back to you, I'll grab some stuff for dinner. Not a takeaway,' he promised. 'I'll cook.'

How could she refuse? It would be such a relief not to have to venture out on such a wild night. 'If you're sure? But I've stuff in the freezer—'

'Please. Let it be my treat, Emma.'

Emma gave an uneasy huff of laughter. 'And you *can* cook?'

'I promise it'll be edible. Just trust me on this, all right?'

Well, she had to, didn't she? Emma thought as she closed the door after him and turned back inside. About dinner and about a lot of other things too.

Declan felt the wind tear at his clothes as he made a dash to his car. But, far from being intimidated by its force, he felt exhilarated, wild, powerful. As if he could do anything he really set his mind to.

If only that were an option.

Following Emma's directions, he soon found his way to the row of neatly kept cottages and drove slowly along until he found Cedric Dutton's.

Hefting his case off the passenger seat, he swung out of his car. Making his way to the front door, Declan lifted his hand and banged loudly. When there was no response, he called, 'Mr Dutton? I'm a doctor from the Kingsholme surgery. I'd like a word. Could you let me in, please?'

Declan waited and listened and, finally, there was a shuffling inside and the door was opened just a crack. Two faded blue eyes under bushy brows looked suspiciously out. 'Who're you?'

'I'm a doctor from the Kingsholme surgery,' Declan repeated. 'May I come in?'

A beat of silence while the elderly man digested the information. 'No law against it, I suppose,' he said, unlocking the chain and holding the door open.

Once inside, Declan extended his hand. 'Declan O'Malley, Mr Dutton.'

'New around here, are you?' Cedric looked over the imposing male figure while he held Declan's hand in a fragile grip.

'Yes. I'm in partnership with Dr Armitage.' Unobtrusively, Declan watched his patient's general mobility as Cedric led the way back inside to the lounge room.

It took a little time for the elderly man to settle himself into his armchair. 'So—why did you want to see me?' he asked, seeming to sense the importance of Declan's visit. 'That girl's being talking to you, I'll bet?'

'Libby Macklin is a Registered Nurse, Mr Dutton. It's part of her job to check on our senior patients. We depend on her to tell us how your health is. She was concerned for you and she's a skilled professional, otherwise, she wouldn't be employed at our practice. You should have let her check you over.'

'Maybe.' Cedric shrugged a skinny shoulder.

'How's your general health, Cedric?' Declan's voice was gentle. He didn't want to antagonize his new patient from the outset.

'Days get a bit long. I'm not as fit as I used to be.'

'I understand that. What about your exercises?' Declan asked. 'Are you doing them? You know they're essential to help your muscles recover from the stroke.'

The elderly man hesitated. 'Sometimes I do them. But it's hard when everything's crook…'

'I know.'

Cedric looked sceptical. 'What would you know about it—young fella like you?'

Declan snorted a hard laugh. 'Oh, believe me, Cedric, I know.' Briefly, Declan explained something of his own circumstances.

'I get a bit *down*,' Cedric admitted. 'Like you said—'

'Depression is all part of the syndrome.' Declan leaned forward, his hands linked between his knees. 'When your body won't do what you want it to, you feel robbed of self-respect. And it's hard when you lose everything you could once be sure of.'

'My word, that's it!' Cedric looked impressed. 'For a while there I couldn't even get my pants on.' His mouth compressed in a reluctant grin. 'Or do up any buttons. And shoelaces were a lost cause.'

Declan nodded sympathetically. 'Was it explained to you just what a stroke is?'

'Something about a blood clot, isn't it?'

'Exactly. A stroke happens when a clot blocks a blood vessel or artery in the brain. It interrupts the blood flow and suddenly the body is out of whack.'

'Like damming a river,' Cedric acknowledged thoughtfully. 'I never cottoned on. But I do now you've explained it.'

'So you can see why those exercises are so important, can't you?'

'Reckon I can.' Cedric thought long and hard. 'So, this Libby, the nurse, she could help me with that, could she?'

'Yes.' Declan nodded. 'But I want you to come into the hospital one day a week for the next while and see our regular physiotherapist, Michelle Crother. I'll arrange transport for you.'

Cedric sighed resignedly. 'I suppose that'd be the thing to do.'

While he had Cedric's tacit acceptance of the changes he wanted to implement, Declan thought he'd push gently ahead with another suggestion. 'What about getting back into a bit of social life? Do you play cards?'

'I don't mind a game or two.'

'Then you might enjoy coming along to the seniors' club.' Since his involvement with Carolyn Jones, Declan had done his homework and clued himself in on what was available to the older residents of the town. 'They meet regularly on a Wednesday at the farmers' hall and the CWA provide lunch. From what I hear, it's a friendly group. They'd make you welcome.' Declan grinned disarmingly. 'You'd possibly know most of them anyway, an old-timer like you.'

'Probably would.' Cedric looked down at his hands. 'I lost touch a bit when I had the stroke...'

'So, how's your appetite?' Declan infused enthusiasm into his voice, sensing Cedric was apt to drift off into introspection. 'Are you managing with the meals on wheels?'

'Food's OK.' Cedric shrugged. 'Sometimes I don't feel like eating much.'

'Once we can get you out and about a bit more, all that will improve. Get yourself out into the sun as well. That will keep up your vitamin D requirement. Very important, whatever our age.'

Cedric nodded, taking it all on board. Then he lifted his eyebrows in a query. 'What did you say your name was, Doctor?'

'O'Malley. Call me Declan. I'll be your medical officer from now on, if you're agreeable?'

'You seem all right,' Cedric said grudgingly. 'Not bossy like some.'

Like the women, Declan interpreted wryly. But at least he'd made headway with this old man. Stirred him up enough to take an interest in his own welfare. And that felt surprisingly good. 'Now—' Declan flipped open his medical case '—how would you feel about me checking you over while I'm here?'

'Fair enough, I suppose.' Cedric looked around him with agitation. 'Where do you want me?'

'Just there's fine.' Declan slung his stethoscope around his neck and grinned. 'And I promise I'll keep the prodding to a minimum.'

* * *

Emma's heartbeat was thrumming. Surely he'd be here soon. It seemed ages since he'd left to visit his patient. An age in which she'd had a leisurely bath and dressed in comfortable trousers and a fine woollen black top. She'd brushed her hair and left it loose and kept her make-up to a minimum.

Why was she fussing so? They were simply sharing a meal. He'd probably prefer to eat in the kitchen. But then, perhaps she should make the evening special and set the small table in the dining room. Would that look a bit contrived? He'd hate that. Although, just in case, she'd go ahead and light the fire in the dining room…

Finally, a knock sounded at her front door.

'Hi.' Hands occupied with his shopping bags, Declan leaned forward and planted a lingering kiss on her mouth when Emma opened the door. 'Sorry, I'm a bit late. It's a wild night out there. I nearly got blown to bits.'

'Hello…' Emma said when she could breathe again. The touch of his mouth had sent up sparks. She wanted to stop him right there, wrap her arms around his body and just *hold* him. She wanted him. So much. But he was already at the worktop unloading his shopping. 'What are we having?' she asked, peering over his shoulder.

He tipped his head on one side and grinned

down at her. 'Char-grilled spiced lamb cutlets with ratatouille.'

Emma gurgled a soft laugh. In other words, grilled chops and vegetables. 'I'm impressed.'

'You're not.' He sent her an indulgent half-amused look. 'But give me my moment of fame here.'

'What can I do to help?'

'Ah—' he indicated the array of vegetables he'd bought—red and yellow peppers, zucchini and vine tomatoes. 'These have to be cut into bite-sized pieces.'

'Even though we're starving hungry?'

'Even though.' Declan gently elbowed her out of the way to select a knife from the kitchen block. 'Just do what the main man tells you, please? It'll be worth the wait.'

Emma was still chuckling to herself as she set about her task. Since he was going to so much trouble to feed her, she definitely *would* set the table in the dining room.

They took a long time over dinner, as though neither of them wanted it to end. 'How did I do, then?' Declan asked finally.

Emma smiled. He'd given her a look so warm, she'd felt its impact skidding and sliding across her nerves and along her backbone before settling in a swirling mass in her belly. 'You did so well, I just might have to keep you. This was such a good idea,' she rushed on. 'To have dinner at home.'

'Yes, it was.' Declan's gaze shimmered over her face and then roamed to register the gleam of lamplight that threw her tawny lashes into sharp relief against her flushed cheeks. He moved a bit uncomfortably as his body zinged to a new awareness. He took a careful mouthful of his wine, his eyes caressing her over the rim of his glass. He ached to touch her intimately, to breathe in the sweet scent of her silky hair, stroke the softness of her naked body as she lay next to him…

'Coffee?' Emma felt a quicksilver flip in her stomach. She'd been aware of his overt scrutiny.

'Not for me, thanks.'

She swung to her feet. 'I'll clear the table and stack the dishwasher, then.' She sent him a quick smile. 'Go through to the lounge. We'll be more comfortable in there.'

Declan extinguished the candles they'd used on the dinner table and then crossed the hallway to the lounge room. He went to stand at the window, drawing back the curtains slightly in order to check the state of the weather himself. In the glow from the street lights he could see the trees bending, their foliage swirling into a mad dance in the wake of the wind's rushing passage.

He turned when Emma came in. 'How long do you think the storm will take to get here?' He opened his arms in invitation and she slid into his embrace.

'I'm no expert.' Emma rested her head against his shoulder. 'But I'd rather be here than out driving somewhere—wouldn't you?'

'That's a no-brainer,' he said. 'Of course I'd rather be here.' He looked down at her. 'That's if it's all right if I hang about?'

'I'd have turfed you out ages ago if it wasn't.'

Declan gave one of his lazy smiles. 'Would I have gone, though?'

'Of course you would.' Emma stroked the tips of her fingers across the small of his back, her hands already addicted to the sensation. 'You're an old-fashioned kind of guy.'

Declan looked pained. 'Are you saying my clothes need an update?'

Emma's mouth widened in a grin. They were shadow dancing again—fooling around, as if it was obvious to both of them that if their conversation became too serious, too personal, then anything could happen...'Stop fishing for compliments,' she said. 'You know you dress very well.'

'I undress very well, too,' he rejoined daringly.

Emma's heart twanged out of rhythm. 'Do you?'

'Mmm.' Declan registered the tiny swallow in her throat. 'So,' he said softly, moving so that his hands rested on the tops of her arms and feeling the tremble that went through her, 'what do you want to do with the rest of the evening?'

Emma opened her mouth and closed it again, knowing deep in her heart that this was a moment of no return. Was she ready? Were *they* ready? They'd never know unless they put their trust in one another, reached out and gathered life in. 'You could stay—if you like…?'

His eyes locked with hers, dark in shadow, tender in their caress. 'My whole body aches with wanting you, Emma. As long as you're sure?'

'Yes.' He should have come into her life sooner, but he was here now. And that was all that mattered. 'Yes.' She looked at him and smiled, feeling the weight of indecision drop from her like an unwanted heavy garment. 'I've never been more sure of anything.'

Declan made a deep sound in his throat that could have been a sigh. Then he drew her close, lowering his mouth to claim her lips.

That was all it took. Like a spark on straw, the fire of their passion took hold and in a breath it was raging.

Declan whispered harshly against her mouth. 'I meant to take it slow…'

She arched back with a little cry. 'No—not slow.' Her hands threaded through his hair and she trapped his face, holding him. 'I need you, Declan—'

He turned his head and gently nipped the soft flesh below her thumb, his eyes pinpoints of desire when she gasped an indrawn breath. 'Which bedroom?'

'Mine.'

Clothes flew off in a flurry, Declan swearing over a leg of his jeans that refused to leave his foot. Finally, he stepped back and stared at her. At the tendrils of corn-silk hair draping gently on to her creamy naked shoulders. At the swanlike grace-fulness of her neck. At the small line of muscle delineating the length of her upper arm. The sweet roundness of her breasts. The shallow dip of her tummy…'Emma—' He felt his voice catch on a painful swallow. 'You're—' He shook his head. 'You're beautiful.'

'And you…' She hardly realized what she was doing, reaching out to slide her fingers down over his diaphragm, over his belly and dip into the shallow nook of his navel.

Suddenly, Declan made a gravelly sound of protest, jamming his hand over hers to stop its movement. 'Wait…' He looked around blankly and then hooked up his jeans, slipping a tiny packet from the back pocket. 'I never know whether there's a right time to do this,' he growled.

Emma felt herself blushing, crossing her arms tightly across her ribcage. He'd turned his back and she could see the shallow hollow just above the base of his spine. A tiny jagged laugh left her mouth. 'No need for diagrams, Declan—just do it…'

Oh, God…it was like stumbling into paradise. He touched her teasingly, his hands light and seductive in their rhythm. Instinctively, he knew what would please her, excite her, bring her to the brink but not quite tip over.

Emma was wild for him, a wildness she'd never known, drawing him closer, feeling him hover at the core of her femininity before plunging in. She gasped, dragging him in more deeply, her head arching back as she called his name, feeling the sweet ripeness of her release gathering and then splintering her into a thousand pieces. Her name exploded on Declan's tongue as his climax followed hers a millisecond later, their hearts thumping a wild tattoo as they fell back to earth.

After a long time, they pulled back from each other, two sets of bruised lips, two pairs of eyes hazed with a new kind of wonderment.

'So…' he said.

'So,' she echoed huskily.

Lifting a hand, he knuckled her cheek gently. 'Why did we wait so long?'

CHAPTER EIGHT

EMMA had no time to answer.

'I don't believe this!' Declan's expletive hit the air as his mobile rang. 'Can't we get two minutes to call our own?'

'Where's your phone?' Emma was out of bed and reaching for her gown.

'Pocket of my jeans.'

'Here.' She hooked them off the floor and tossed them to him. It had to be an emergency some-where. She knew that instinctively.

They had trouble, the police sergeant, Gary Bryson, informed Declan. Part of the roof at the farmers' hall had blown off. The hall had been packed with the usual Friday bingo players. There was confusion, to say the least. No one was sure about injuries but could the doctors come? Declan closed off his phone and in clipped terms relayed the message to Emma.

'Right.' She snatched up her own mobile off the bedside table. 'I'll get on to the hospital and alert them we might be sending patients in. They'll automatically recall any staff who are available.'

'Let's just be grateful the power lines haven't gone down,' Declan said as they dressed hurriedly.

'Don't count your chickens quite yet,' Emma warned. 'But at least the hospital has a backup power supply. It'll kick in if the worst happens.'

Declan grunted a non-reply, looking broodingly at Emma as she twisted her hair quickly into a ponytail. A frown touched his eyes. He felt as though he'd been catapulted from a delicious dream with no time to wallow in its aftermath. But he could still smell Emma's perfume, still feel the softness of her skin beneath his hands.

His mouth tightened. He wanted more and he couldn't have it. They'd taken a huge step into the unknown tonight. They'd needed time and closeness to talk about it, wind down, make love again, this time slowly, softly, sexily—

'Your top's inside out,' Emma said, breaking his thought pattern.

Impatiently, Declan dragged the T-shirt over his head and rectified it. 'The timing's all wrong for this, Emma.'

Well, she knew that. Emma's head was bent as she pulled on a pair of sturdy boots. But they were rural doctors. They had to attend. Emergencies didn't choose their time to happen. Heaven knew what they'd find when they got to the hall. And she didn't want to be doing this any more than Declan. The timing *was* all wrong. She'd wanted a blissful few hours with him. Their newness as lovers surely demanded that. She'd wanted to hold him and have him hold her and just *talk*. About nothing. About everything. But it seemed as though an unkind fate had stepped in and now her emotions were all over the place. Declan's too, if she was a betting woman. She popped upright from the edge of the bed. 'Ready?'

They went in Declan's car. Halfway to the hall the street lights flickered and faded and the night around them was plunged into darkness.

'I've a couple of lantern torches in the boot' was Declan's only comment.

The rain had started in earnest by the time they got to the hall. 'Let's proceed with caution,' Declan warned, handing Emma one of the torches and taking the other himself.

'We should go through the front entrance,' she said. 'It seems the least affected.' To her relief, the State Emergency Services people were already on the scene, their bright orange overalls lending a sense of security. Emergency lighting was rapidly being put in place. 'That's John Cabot, the team leader for the SES,' she told Declan. 'We'll speak to him first.'

Introductions were made swiftly and Declan asked the question on both their minds, 'What's the damage, John? Do we know yet?'

'Less than we feared, Doc. Most of the folk had already left. Just a few stragglers having a last cuppa, from what we know. The roof over the rear of the hall has pretty much gone but the rest seems intact. I've a couple of guys up there presently checking and getting tarpaulins into place to keep out the rain. Let us know if you need more lighting.'

'Thanks, John.' Declan nodded, taking it all in. 'We'll let you get on with it, then.'

'Oh, look—' Emma made a dash forward. 'There's Moira! What on earth is she doing here?'

'I'm on the driving roster for our seniors' group at the church,' Moira explained agitatedly. 'And I'd just come to collect them when the roof went. This is Agnes—' She indicated the elderly lady slumped in a chair beside them. 'I think she's hurt quite badly,' Moira added in a frightened whisper.

Declan had already sized up the situation. His seeking gaze went quickly around the hall. 'Moira, is there a first aid room or somewhere we could make Agnes more comfortable?'

'Er—yes—yes…' Moira visibly pulled herself together, pointing to a room at the side of the hall. 'And, mercifully, it's still intact.'

'Over here!' Declan hailed the two ambulances officers who had just arrived and explained what he needed.

'Take it easy,' he instructed as they settled the elderly woman on the narrow bunk bed. Agnes looked glassily pale against the deep purple of her cardigan. 'Can you tell us what happened, Agnes?' he asked gently as he began his examination.

'Sitting at the table…' Agnes moistened her lips slowly. 'Something hit me—fell forward—hard, terrible hard…'

'That must have hurt, Agnes.' Emma held her hand to the injured woman's wrist. 'Thready,' she reported softly.

Declan replaced his stethoscope. 'Let's step outside for a minute.'

'What's the matter with me?' Agnes asked fretfully.

'It'll be all right, dear.' Moira took the older woman's hand and held it. 'The doctors will look after you.'

Emma followed Declan out of the room. 'What do you think?' she asked quietly.

'Hard to tell, but she could have a splenic hae-matoma. She'll need a CT scan asap.'

'We'll send her on, then?'

'Obviously.' Declan gave a dismissive grunt. 'We don't have the equipment to do it here, Emma.'

It was hardly her fault if their little hospital didn't have the advanced facilities of a city radiology department! 'I'll escort Agnes across to the hospital, then,' she said shortly. 'Stabilize her before the road trip to Toowoomba.'

'Do that.' Declan's voice was clipped. 'And call through to Toowoomba, please. Tell them we want a CT scan immediately on arrival. And to make sure they have a supply of O-neg blood ready in case she needs to go to surgery.'

For heaven's sake! Emma's fine chin darted a centimetre upwards. She knew what protocol to follow. Did he ever stop to consider how they'd managed before he'd come? Well, amazingly enough, they had! Then she softened. Giving orders came as naturally to him as breathing. 'Are you worried about a bleed?'

'Without a scanner we can only second-guess.' And it was frustrating him like hell. 'If you'll do the necessary for Agnes, I'll see if there are any more casualties here. So far it looks pretty quiet.'

They went back to the first aid room and Emma explained what they needed to do.

'I'll follow across to the hospital directly, Agnes.' Moira squeezed the older woman's hand. 'Don't worry about a thing.'

'Right, let's get you on board, sweetheart.' The paramedics moved in to make the transfer.

With Moira disappearing out into the night, Declan took a quick look around. Thankfully, the damage was only in one part of the hall. He was still considering the injury to Agnes when he heard his name called. He turned sharply. John Cabot was heading towards him.

'One of my lads has hurt himself, Doc. Breaking all the rules and trying to lift debris on his own.'

'I'll take a look at him.' Declan hitched up his bag and followed the SES leader. 'Who do we have, John?'

'Jason Toohey. One of our local football stars.'

Declan found the young man sitting hunched over, hands crossed, supporting his elbows. 'Where are you hurt, Jason?' Declan hunkered down beside his patient.

'Shoulder.' Jason pulled in a harsh breath. 'Put it out again, I reckon.'

'What do you mean *again*? Does this happen often?'

'I play league, Doc. It's contact sport.'

'I'm well aware of what rugby league is,' Declan muttered. 'I want you over at the hospital so I can look at you properly.'

John Cabot looked on worriedly. 'What do you think, Doc?'

'Shoulder dislocation,' Declan said briefly. He looked about him. 'Is the other ambulance here?'

Gary Bryson joined in the conversation. 'Just heard they've gone to collect a pregnant woman. Roads to Toowoomba are flooded. Looks like she'll have to have the baby here.'

Bendemere didn't take midwifery patients. At least not on a regular basis. But Declan guessed there would be protocol in place for just such an eventuality. And he guessed too that Emma, as usual, would have things well in hand. 'We need to get Jason over to the hospital.'

Rachel Wallace arrived just as Jason was being settled into the treatment room. 'Sorry, guys.' She looked from Declan to the young nursing assistant, Talitha, and made a grimace. 'I'd have been here earlier but when I went to reverse out of the garage, I found a damn great tree had fallen across the driveway. Took me a while to move it.'

Declan's eyes widened ever so slightly. 'You moved a fallen tree on your own?'

'With the help of a chainsaw.' Rachel coughed out a self-deprecating laugh. 'And it was more of a sapling really. But there was no way I could have reversed the car over it. Hi, JT.' She made a sympathetic face at the young man on the treatment couch. 'Is it the shoulder again?'

'Yep.' Jason managed a weak smile, raising his hand in acknowledgment, then wincing as he lowered it quickly.

'Let's get Jason on some oxygen, please,' Declan directed.

'We've all become accustomed to popping Jason's shoulder back in,' Rachel said, adjusting the oxygen. 'Relax now and breathe away, JT. Big tug coming up.'

Not if he could help it, Declan thought. 'I'll just try a manoeuvre here, Rachel,' he informed the nurse manager quietly.

She went to the head of the bed and waited. She watched intently as Declan gently and smoothly reduced Jason's dislocation until his shoulder was safely back in its socket. 'Wow...' Rachel puffed a little breath of admiration. 'You're good.'

Declan's mouth compressed for moment. It was what he'd trained for, for heaven's sake. But nevertheless Rachel's compliment had warmed him like a favourite woolly jumper on a winter's morning. 'Let's get a sling on that arm now, please.'

'Thanks, Doc,' Jason said, perking up. 'Looks like I'll be back in time for the semi-finals week-end after next.'

'No, you won't, old son.' Declan flipped out the patient chart from its rack and took the pen Rachel handed to him. 'You're out for the rest of the season. That shoulder needs resting.'

'Stuff that!' Jason struggled upright, dangling his legs over the side of the treatment couch. 'The team needs me. I play second-row forward.'

'And correct me if I'm wrong.' Declan's tone was professionally detached and even. 'But isn't that the position where you regularly shoulder-charge your opposite number?'

'So?' Jason looked sulky.

'So,' Declan elaborated, 'if you continue play-ing, you'll be lucky if your shoulder's not hanging by a thread by the end of the season. And you'll be very unlikely to have a future in league at all. How old are you, Jason?'

'Nineteen.'

'So, you've plenty of time to get your footy career up and running again.'

Jason gave a howl of dissention.

'Hey, JT, listen to Dr O'Malley, hmm?' Rachel came in with an overbright smile. 'This is his special field of medicine. He knows what he's talking about.'

Jason's lip curled briefly. 'So—what do I have to do, then?' he asked ungraciously.

'I'd like you to have a CAT scan on that shoulder,' Declan said. 'We need to know why it keeps dislocating. In the meantime, chum, it's rest. Want me to have a word with your coach?'

Jason shook his head. 'I'll tell him at training.'

Declan replaced the chart, backing against the treatment couch and folding his arms. 'It won't be the end of the world, Jason.' His tone was gentle. 'We'll make a plan of action when we see the results of your scan. Maybe the problem can be resolved with some appropriate physio. In all probability, you'll be back on the field next season. Call the imaging centre first thing on Monday. They'll give you an appointment. And I'd rather you didn't try to drive, so can you get a lift across to Toowoomba?'

Jason nodded and stood gingerly to his feet. 'Uh—thanks,' he added grudgingly.

'You're welcome, Jason.' Declan's mouth tightened fractionally. 'If you could hang around for a bit, I'll organise a request form for your X-ray.'

'We can fix you up at the nurses' station for that,' Rachel said helpfully. 'And JT, I'm sure you could do with a cup of tea. Or an energy drink, if you'd prefer. Talitha will show you where to go.'

'Follow me.' The young nursing assistant grinned impishly. 'Unless you'd like a wheelchair?'

'No way!' Jason looked horrified. He paused for a second and then, as if he could see he had no other choice, shuffled out after Talitha.

Declan worked his shoulder muscles and lifted his arms in a half-mast stretch.

'Long day?' Rachel commiserated. 'Got time for a hot drink?'

'Perhaps later.' Declan smiled. 'I'll look in on Emma first. See if she needs any backup.'

'Oh—OK, then. I'll be around for a while, if you change your mind.' She sent him a quick grin. 'We'll raid the kitchen.'

'Oh— Hi.' Emma had stepped out of the room that had been quickly rearranged as a delivery suite, to find Declan hovering. She blinked a bit. 'Is something wrong?'

'I came to see if you needed any backup.'

She shook her head. 'We're fine. Dot's a midwife and the baby's well on its way. Shouldn't be any problems.' She looked closely at him and put her hand on his arm. 'You look tired. Why don't you take off? You've a big day tomorrow with Tracey.'

Declan's gaze narrowed. Was she patronizing him? It sure felt like it. His eyes swept over her pale blue hospital gown. 'I'll wait.'

'You don't have to, Declan. I can get a lift home with someone.'

By the time Declan had formulated a reply, she'd turned away and re-entered the delivery room. He had a frown in his eyes as he made his way back to the nurses' station. Damn it! he raged silently. What an awful way for their evening to have turned out.

With the baby boy safely delivered and his mum tidied up, Emma felt a surge of relief. In the little annexe, she stripped off her gown and tossed it into the linen tidy. It had been a very long day. Day and a bit, she realized after a glance at the wall clock. Oh, Lord, she needed her bed. She stretched, feeling the protest of internal muscles, and felt heat rising from her toes upwards until she flushed almost guiltily. She couldn't believe she'd been so wild with Declan, almost frenzied. She stifled a groan. She hoped he'd gone home. She needed time to gather herself. They'd taken a giant step into the unknown. It had seemed the right one at the time but now, in the fuzzy light of the early hours… The smell of coffee, fragrant and rich, drew her towards the hospital kitchen.

And that was where she found her new lover and the nurse manager. All her insecurities from her past relationship, coupled with the most awful kind of disappointment, washed through her like a power-shower of pain. She pulled back, freezing at what she saw—Declan and Rachel were sitting very closely together, their foreheads almost touching, utterly engrossed in quiet conversation. At least Rachel was the one doing the talking, while Declan seemed enthralled, drawn towards her, listening. Emma felt the drum-heavy beat in her chest, the sudden recoil in her stomach. Surely she hadn't misplaced her trust again? Surely…

It was the longest minute of Emma's life. She stood undecided, wanting to run, yet with all her heart wanting to stay. The decision was taken out of her hands when Rachel looked up. 'Emma… hey… Everything OK?'

'Fine.' Emma took a deep breath. 'I smelled coffee.'

'Help yourself.' The nurse manager pressed a strand of auburn hair behind her ear and got to her feet. 'I'm off to crash for a while. I'm on an early.'

Two sets of eyes followed Rachel as she left and then Declan pushed up out of his chair. 'I'll get you a coffee.'

'Don't bother. I've changed my mind.' The words were said tonelessly, like a recorded message.

'Let's get you home, then.' Declan moving with speed, was already ushering her out of the door.

'You seemed very cosy with Rachel back there,' Emma said as they drove. Suddenly she felt she was fighting for her very existence, her emotions unravelling like a ball of string.

'Just killing time,' Declan answered evenly. 'Waiting for you.'

A beat of silence and then, 'I—guess you'd have a lot in common with Rachel. She's worked all over the world in the OR. She's smart and savvy. *And available.*'

'Don't do this, Emma.'

Emma felt her throat thicken. 'She was practically in your lap.'

Declan pulled air into his lungs and let it go. 'Emma, if you're waiting for a reaction, I'm not biting. We just have to accept the evening turned out light years from what we'd hoped for.' He paused. 'What about coming home with me?'

'To the cabin?' He must be out of his mind.

'That's where I call home at the moment.'

'Declan—' Emma made a weary little gesture with her hand '—I'd rather be on my own, if you don't mind.'

'So you can do what?' Declan felt nettled. 'Talk yourself into believing that making love with me was a huge mistake? Or, better still,' he revised with heavy sarcasm, 'that you can't trust me now?'

Emma felt her stomach churn. He was too near the truth for comfort.

Declan gave a fractured sigh and then he spoke quietly. 'I realize you feel vulnerable—hell, don't you think I do as well? But don't blow this up into something it's not, Emma. Come home with me. I'll sleep on the couch. There's hardly anything left of the night, anyway. But at least we'll be together. I hate the thought of you rattling around in that great house on your own.'

'I was doing it long before you came on the scene, Declan. I'm used to it,' she dismissed. 'Besides, the power's back on. I'll be fine.'

With a weary shake of his head, Declan aimed the car towards Kingsholme.

When they turned into the driveway at the surgery, he cut the engine.

Emma's head spun round in query.

'I'll come in with you,' he said. 'Make sure it's all safe—that no water's come in, or worse.'

'Thanks—but there's never been any problem before.'

In other words, I can get along without you very

well; you don't need to come in at all. Declan's hands tightened on the steering wheel. 'It won't take a minute.'

Once inside, Emma stood stiffly in the kitchen, listening as Declan went from room to room, checking things were in order. It seemed only seconds until he was back and poking his head in the door.

'Seems fine, very snug. I'll say goodnight, then.'

'Yes— OK—thanks.' Emma voice sounded thick and vaguely husky.

'I'll be here about eight in the morning,' Declan said. 'To drop the kids off as arranged.'

She nodded. Words, all of them mixed up, tried to force their way from her lips. Words like, *Perhaps I was wrong. Perhaps we need to talk. Can things ever be right between us again?* Instead, she stood there awkwardly. 'Take care on the road back to the cabin.'

Declan's lips twisted in self-mockery. Obviously, she couldn't wait to be shot of his company. He lifted a hand in a stiff kind of farewell but no words came readily to mind. He turned and left quietly.

The next morning, Emma made a concerted effort to corral her private thoughts and concentrate on the children's chatter as they drove to the stables. But it was difficult. Declan had had very little to say when he'd dropped them off—well, nothing personal anyway. But she'd hoped, unrealistically perhaps—? 'There's Jodi waiting for us!' Lauren was beside herself with excitement.

'Now, I want both of you to do exactly what Jodi tells you,' Emma instructed. 'Horses can be a bit tricky.'

Jodi spent some time showing them the basic skills in looking after the horses. 'Now, I'll have to take each of you separately for a ride,' Jodi explained to the children. 'Lauren, you can go first. Joel, you'll have to wait a bit, OK?'

'I don't wanna ride.' Joel tugged his cap further down on his forehead. 'I'd rather help feed the horses.'

'Right, you're easily pleased.' Jodi grinned. 'Come with me, then, dude.'

Jodi was back in a few minutes and began saddling a chestnut pony. 'This is Lady Marmalade,' she told an entranced Lauren. She showed the little girl how to mount and then positioned her feet in the stirrups. 'Lady has a soft mouth,' Jodi explained as Lauren took up the reins. 'That means she'll go exactly where you want her to with just a touch on the bridle.'

Watching on, Emma said, 'Thanks for doing all this, Jodi.'

'No worries.' Jodi gave a dimple-bright grin. 'It's good for kids to learn to be safe around animals and have fun while they're doing it. All set?' She looked up at her young charge. 'I'll lead Lady for a while until you get used to sitting on her back and then I might let you have a ride by yourself.'

Lauren's little face was alight with happiness.

Jodi pointed to the paddock adjoining the track. 'Now, for starters, we'll be taking Lady over there.'

Lauren small hands clutched the reins, her thin little shoulders almost stiff with anticipation of her first riding lesson.

Jodi looked a question at Emma. 'Coming along?'

'I thought perhaps I should keep an eye on Joel.'

'He'll be fine.' Jodi flapped a hand. 'He's with the guys. And there's a new puppy over at the barn. He'll have fun with him. Isn't it a gorgeous morning after the storm?' Jodi chatted light-heartedly as they made their way towards the big paddock.

Emma began to feel her spirits lighten. It was indeed a lovely morning. The sun had risen, dispersing the mist, and a brilliant burst of gold-tipped fingers spanned the horizon.

Lauren was going beautifully, Emma decided and, even though she didn't know terribly much about riding in general, she could see the little girl was a natural. Already her seat was easy, her little back straight, her body moving in tune with the pony's rhythmic gait. She watched as Jodi gave a thumbs-up sign and then stepped away, leaving Lauren in charge of her mount. With a tap of her heels, Lauren urged Lady forward and the pony responded, picking up her pace into a bouncy brisk walk.

Emma thought the smile on the child's face would have dimmed even the Christmas lights. Oh, sweetheart, Emma's heart swelled. I wish your mum could see you now. She'd be back home in a flash.

And then it happened.

A black streak in the form of a wilful, naughty puppy tore across the paddock in front of Lady. Without warning, the pony took fright, breaking into a jerky canter and racing through the grass. Lauren cried out…and so did Emma.

Jodi began sprinting to try to contain the pony but Lady was having none of it.

'Oh, no!' Emma's hand went to her heart as

Lauren lost her seat and tumbled to the ground. Emma ran as if she was possessed. Lauren was in a little heap on the ground, hunched over and looking into the distance at the pony that had careened away to the far side of the paddock. 'Is she hurt?' Emma skidded to a stop and dropped to the ground beside the child.

'She landed like a pro.' Jodi had her arm around Lauren. 'She's one smart little girl.'

'Ooh…' Emma felt a sob of relief in her chest.

'I fell off,' Lauren said as though the fact amazed her.

'Yes, you did.' Jodi squeezed her shoulders. 'I did too when I first began to ride.'

'Did you?' Lauren looked a wide-eyed question at her mentor.

'Broke my wrist.' Jodi held up a strong, straight arm. 'But you'd never know now, would you?'

Lauren shook her head. 'I don't think I broke anything.'

'Just let me take a little look at you, Lauren.' Emma bent to the child. She did a quick neuro check and asked Lauren to turn her head and lift her arms. 'Now, can you squeeze my fingers really hard? Good girl. Now, stand up for me, Lauren. And walk a straight line, please, sweetheart. Good. That's lovely.' Emma's heart fell back into its rightful place.

'I'll go and catch Lady.' Jodi scrambled upright. 'And we'll get her back to the stables.'

'Can I ride her back?' a now recovered Lauren asked eagerly.

Emma looked doubtful but Jodi said, 'If you feel up to it, Lauren—of course you can. But I'll lead her, just to make sure she doesn't get up to any more tricks.'

The ride ended with no more mishaps. 'I'll collect Joel now,' Emma said. 'And we'll get out of your hair.'

'Don't be silly,' Jodi dismissed. 'Mrs McGinty's invited us up to the house for morning tea. She loves kids—and company.'

'We can stay, can't we, Emma?' Lauren pleaded.

How could she refuse the child? 'Well, I guess it would be rather rude if we didn't,' Emma gave in gracefully.

'Good.' Jodi looked well pleased. 'Let's round up young Joel.'

Lauren skipped ahead.

'You will let them come again, won't you, Emma?' Jodi asked as the two young women made their way slowly across to the barn. 'Lauren's little mishap was just that. I would never have put her on a pony that was unsafe.'

Emma managed a little smile. 'I'm not sure just

how long the children will be staying with me but, while they are, I guess if you can manage the strain then I can too.'

CHAPTER NINE

EMMA was glad she'd had the distraction of the children's company throughout the day. But now it was almost nine o'clock and the long night stretched ahead of her.

She felt too restless to watch television, her thoughts too fragmented to read. And sleep was out of the question.

She wandered aimlessly about the kitchen. She could probably do some meal preparation for next week. Perhaps freeze some simple meals for the kids. When the firm rap sounded on her back door, her heart slammed into her ribcage with such force she had to gulp down her next breath.

It had to be Declan. No one else was likely to be banging on her kitchen door at this time of night. Like water draining out of a bath, the tension trickled out of her shoulders and the knots in her stomach began to loosen. Thank heaven he'd come. Now, she could apologise for her crazy reaction last night and they could get back on an even keel again. So simple when you thought about it.

Declan waited for Emma to answer the door. Physically, he was wiped. His eyes felt as if they'd been back-filled with fine sand sprinkled with wood ash and hisguts knitted into a tight uneasy series of knots. He lifted his shoulders in a huge controlling breath. Hell, would she even let him in?

In an agitated gesture, Emma wiped her hands down the sides of her jeans and went to open the door. She raised her gaze, looking out on to the lighted verandah. 'Declan...' Her voice shook and suddenly her limbs felt as though they were being held together by string. He looked dark and achingly familiar in his black sweater. His hair was mussed as though his fingers had run through it over and over and light stubble sprinkled his jaw and chin.

'This couldn't wait until surgery on Monday,' he said. 'May I come in?'

Emma held the door wide open.

Declan walked into the kitchen and then spun to face her. 'I thought, as you're temporary guardian of Tracey's children, you'd need to know how things went today.'

Emma felt the impact of his words right down in her gut. It wasn't what she'd expected to hear at all. And he was being so formal—as if they were medical partners and nothing more. Was that what he wanted? Had she ruined everything? She said the first thing that came into her head. 'Have you eaten?'

Declan rubbed his forehead with a long finger. 'Nev and I stopped for a bite on the way home. A coffee would be good, though–if you wouldn't mind,' he added, as if unsure of her response.

'Of course I don't mind. Sit down.'

'Kids in bed?' Declan dropped on to a chair at the head of the scrubbed pine table.

'Ages ago.' With her back towards him, Emma drew in a few calming breaths and set water to boil. She got down mugs and instant coffee and stood them on the bench. 'We had a very full day,' she said, shaking the contents of a packet of chocolate biscuits on to a plate.

'Oh, yes. How did the riding go?'

'A bit mixed.' She laughed jaggedly and filled him in. Then the jug boiled and she made the coffee, added milk and took it across to the table.

'Lauren's OK, though?' Declan took up his coffee mug and looked at her over its rim.

'Took it entirely in her stride. She wants to go back again and Jodi's happy to give her some riding lessons.'

'Good.' Declan drank his coffee slowly, looking into space, almost as if he'd run out of words.

A silence, awkward.

'How was Tracey, then?'

Declan brought his gaze up sharply. 'Things are still a bit iffy between her and Carolyn.'

'Well, they were never going to fall into each other's arms.'

'How naïve of me.' He gave a grunt of mirthless laughter. 'I was actually hoping they might have. I guess I'll never understand women.'

Emma recognized his response as a not too subtle dig at her own recent behaviour and swallowed any comeback she might have made. Instead, she'd stay entirely professional. 'How was Adam when he saw his mum?'

'A bit quiet. Tracey had some one-to-one time with him later in the day and they seemed much more in tune with each other by the end of it.'

'He's been a lost little boy,' Emma said quietly. 'So—has the family come up with any plan for the future—or even if there's to be one?'

'I'm not about to let Tracey slip through the cracks,' Declan said emphatically.

'You can't be all things to all people,' Emma reminded him.

After a long, assessing kind of look at her, Declan lifted his mug and drained the last of his coffee. 'I've arranged some joint counselling for the family. And Nev's come up with a kind of plan. He's going to try to persuade Carolyn to take a holiday with her sister at the Gold Coast.'

'So, Tracey could come back home without Carolyn peering over her shoulder?' Emma caught on quickly.

'It could work,' he justified.

'Small steps, then?'

'Better than none at all,' Declan said and got to his feet.

Emma swung upright after him. 'You'll keep me in the loop about Lauren and Joel, won't you?'

Declan scrubbed his hands across his face in a weary gesture. 'That goes without saying.' He moved towards the door. 'I'll get going, then.'

Emma's heart beat fast. If she didn't speak now, she had a terrible feeling the opportunity she sought would be lost for ever. 'I'm sorry about last night.'

Declan went very still. 'What part of it are you sorry about, Emma?'

Oh, dear God—what on earth was he thinking—that she regretted making love with him? Goosebumps ran up her backbone. 'Could we talk—properly?' Emma didn't miss his cautious look, nor the way he seemed to gather himself in.

'I guess an opportunity might present itself next week.'

'Next week?' Emma echoed stupidly. Then she thought—perhaps this is his way of breaking things off? Well, this time she intended fighting for what she believed in. And she believed in *them*. 'I—thought perhaps tomorrow?'

Declan felt the strength drain out of his legs. He'd been convinced it was never going to work between them. That Emma, for her own reasons, didn't want it to work. He swallowed deeply. 'You have the children.'

'I'll ask Moira to come over and stay with them. She won't mind...'

'OK.' Declan spread his hands in a shrug. 'Would you like to meet somewhere or—'

'No,' Emma cut in. 'I'll come to you. I should make it by afternoon.'

'Fine.' he nodded. 'Just one thing, Emma.'

'Yes?'

What could have passed for the flicker of a smile crossed his mouth. 'Don't bring food.'

Declan couldn't keep still. When would she get here? She hadn't specified a time. He'd been for a run, had a shower and a badly needed shave. 'For crying out loud, just get here...' he intoned softly. Already Emma Armitage had stirred such powerful feelings in him; she was so sweet and funny. Sexy. But did she want a future with him? The thought that she might not made nerves tighten low in his belly. He stopped his train of thought.

It would be dusk soon. He slid a look at his watch and took a deep breath. He was on a knife-edge, his emotions seesawing from high to low and back. In the quiet still of late afternoon, he heard her car long before he saw it. His heart gave an extra thud as he hurried outside to wait for her.

Emma had steeled herself for a great deal of awkwardness when she and Declan faced each other. Little speeches, none of them right, ran through her head. And she had to face the fact that he hadn't seemed in any hurry for this conversation they had to have.

She drove slowly towards the cabin. She was going to her lover—wild for just the sight of him, the touch of him. Oh, Lord—her heart was hammering as she brought the car to a stop. Did he still want *her*?

Well, she'd never find out by sitting here. Throwing open the door of her car, she swung out.

Declan was standing there. Waiting.

'Hi,' she croaked.

'I thought you'd never get here.' His gaze snapped over her.

'Moira got held up.'

'Not literally?'

'No.' A ghost of a smile crossed her lips. 'Just a domestic drama.' She wanted to reach up and touch his newly shaven jaw, place her hands on his chest, but felt too held back by the air of tension running between them. She swallowed nervously. 'Are you OK?'

He gave a tight little smile. 'Dunno yet.'

'Oh—'

Declan saw the pitch and roll of emotion in her eyes. The uncertainty. Oh, hell. He didn't want to put her through the wringer like this. He spoke quietly into the stillness. 'Would you like a hug in the meantime?'

She nodded. 'Please...'

He closed the space between them in one swift move and gathered her in.

Emma felt herself melt into his arms, the familiar ache, the quivering in her stomach. She could have happily stayed there for ever.

'What are we going to do about this, Emma?' Declan asked, his voice a little rough around the edges. 'We seem to be going in circles.'

Emma's heart gave a sickening lurch. She pulled back, her hands creeping up to rest on his shoulders. 'The whole weekend's been manic. I've been wanting to talk but we haven't seemed able to connect.'

'No.'

'I never meant to hurt you, Declan.'

'In my heart of hearts, I knew that.' He lifted a hand, his knuckles brushing softly over her cheek.

'Thank you.' His kiss came seconds later, a long exquisite shiver of a kiss that twined through her body languidly like smoke haze. The tenderness and delicacy of the simple union of their lips left her shaky and she nestled into him, holding him closer.

When they finally pulled away, Declan kept his arms loosely around her. She slowly opened her eyes. They gleamed. But they asked him questions as well. 'Let's go in,' he said, his voice rough with emotion. His fingers slid down her arm, dragging through hers, and they made their way inside. 'Make yourself comfortable,' he said. 'Something to drink?'

'No, I'm fine, thanks.' Emma curled herself into the corner of the soft, cushiony settee.

Declan looked about him and then, because anything else would have seemed ridiculous, he parked beside her, stretching his arms along the back. He looked a question at her as much as to say, *Well, let's hear it.*

Very aware of him beside her, Emma bit gently at her bottom lip. He seemed ill at ease, although he was pretending not to. There was definitely an air of vulnerability about him. 'About what happened at the hospital—'

'When you all but cut me dead.'

She made a little gesture with her hand. 'None of this has been easy from the start, Declan. You landed on me out of nowhere. Took me over—'

'On the contrary. We agreed on a course of action for the practice.'

Her mind a whirlpool of jumbled thoughts and emotions, Emma said starkly, 'I just wonder if you'll stay, Declan.'

'That's not a decision for now.' His voice tightened and there was a long pause. 'You don't trust me at all, do you, Emma?'

'It's the circumstances we're in I don't trust. I see how frustrated you get with the shortcomings of working in a rural practice. Friday night with Agnes, for instance.'

'Guilty as charged.' His mouth pulled down. 'But that's nothing to do with my personal relationship with you.'

Emma's heart was pounding, uncertainty spreading to every part of her body. 'It has everything to do with it, Declan.' She blinked rapidly. 'If you walk away, then I'll have left myself open to hurt again.'

'Aren't you even willing to try? When we could have something good and true between us?'

She gave a bitter little laugh. 'I thought I had something good and true with Marcus.'

At his growl of dissent, Emma shook her head. 'I know it sounds pathetic but everything just imploded when I saw you and Rachel together. I was seeing Marcus and Bree again and I suppose I overreacted.'

'Just a bit.' Declan looked at her narrowly. 'How well do you know Rachel?'

She seemed surprised at the question. 'Professionally, quite well. Personally, I guess not that well.'

'So you don't know she's facing something of a personal crisis.'

Emma's eyes widened in alarm. 'Is she ill?'

'No. You're aware some time ago Rachel spent several tours of duty with Médicins Sans Frontières?'

'Doctors Without Borders—yes I knew that. She was a theatre nurse. Dad always said she was brilliant.'

Declan lifted a shoulder. 'Apparently, during her time abroad, Rachel had a long-term relationship with one of the surgeons, Ethan O'Rourke. They were planning to marry on their next leave. But it never happened because he was killed in some kind of tribal skirmish. Rachel got out and came home.'

'That's so sad.' Emma's hand went to her heart.

Declan continued, 'It was always Ethan's dream to have a properly equipped OR at the hospital where they worked. Now, it seems, his parents have gathered enough funds and support to make it happen. They want Rachel to go back and over-see its setting-up.'

Several wild thoughts juxtaposed in Emma's head. Her nerves tightened alarmingly. Had Rachel asked Declan to go with her? With his medical background, it would seem a feasible request. The implication struck her as painfully as fists.

'You said there was a problem?'

'Rachel doesn't want to go.'

'So, why did she need to speak to you about it?'

'She wanted an objective opinion.'

'I see…and what did you tell her?'

'I told her to follow her instincts.'

Emma nodded and felt relief sweep through her. 'Rachel's a strong person. She'll stand by whatever she decides. It will be the hospital's loss if she goes, though.'

'Another problem we don't need to solve just now.' Declan gave her a long look. 'Nothing's black and white, Emma. We're all just muddling along. But sometimes you have to take a chance. To trust someone other than yourself.'

'You're talking about us, aren't you?' She had a lump in her throat. 'I want to try—'

'But you're afraid?'

She nodded bleakly.

Oh, Emma…' He made a rough sound in his throat and opened his arms wide.

'Come here…'

On a little broken cry, she scooted up the settee and straight into his arms. They held each other tightly for a very long time, until Declan broke the silence with, 'Feel better now?'

She gave a shaky smile and touched a finger to the smooth skin at his throat where his shirt lay unbuttoned. 'You sound like my doctor.'

'I am your doctor,' he answered softly. 'If you want me to be?'

Her gaze faltered. 'I hate it when we're not friends.'

His fingers, blunt and strong, tipped her chin up gently so that she met his gaze. 'How long can you stay?'

He'd spoken so quietly, his voice so deep it made her shiver. 'Not as long as I'd like to,' she murmured, raising her hands, spreading her fingers to bracket his face. 'We could kiss and make up a bit, though…'

Their mouths sought each other's, then sipped and nipped and she heard a half growl escape from his throat as their kiss deepened. Was there time for what she really wanted? To make love again with him was what she really wanted. Needed.

Instead, she felt Declan pulling back, his fingers moving to twine in her hair at the back. The gentlest pressure brought her head up. His eyes were disturbingly intent as they looked into her face. 'Emma...' His throat worked as he swallowed. 'I want you. But not like this. Hurried and under pressure because you have to go. When we make love again, I want it to be long and leisurely. Slow. Very slow and with all the time in the world afterwards. You understand, don't you?'

'I suppose...' She felt her head drop a little. 'There will *be* a time, won't there?'

'I give you my word,' he said huskily, nudging a strand of her hair sideways, seeking the soft skin at her nape. 'Even if we have to close the surgery and fly the coop to accomplish it.'

'I can just see Moira's face if we did that!'

'I'm not so sure,' he countered with a lazy grin. 'Moira's a canny soul. I think she'd probably give us her tick of approval and reschedule all our appointments.'

* * *

On Monday morning, Declan popped his head into Emma's consulting room. 'Good morning.' His mouth tweaked at the corners. 'Sleep well?'

'Fine, thanks.'

'Good.' They exchanged a very private smile. 'Me too. Er...' He lifted a hand and pressed it to the back of his neck. 'Quick team meeting before surgery?'

'Now?'

'Please.'

'OK.' Emma left what she doing and went with him along to the staff kitchen.

'This is just to pull a few things together before the week gets away from us,' Declan explained to the assembled group.

'Before we start, Declan,' Moira said, 'what's the latest on Agnes? They won't tell me anything at the hospital except the standard response.'

'Sorry about that, Moira. I should have got back to you,' Declan apologized. 'Agnes has settled quite nicely. At this stage they don't think they'll have to operate. And I believe some family members from Brisbane arrived yesterday to be with her.'

'Oh, that is good news.' Moira picked up her cup of tea and held it against her chest. 'How long will she be in, do we know?'

'Not sure. I wouldn't think the hospital will be in any hurry to discharge her, though.'

'In that case, I'll send some flowers.'

'Better still, Moira, make the flowers from all of us and charge them to the practice,' Declan said. 'I think the place can stand the cost for one of our senior citizens.'

'That's a nice gesture,' Emma said quietly.

'I'm a nice guy,' Declan joked.

Emma laughed huskily, trying to hide the sudden leap in her pulse as his thigh brushed against hers. 'What else is on the agenda?' she got out quickly before her thoughts became entirely scrambled.

Declan sent her a wry smile. He knew what he'd *like* to be on the agenda. Instead, he snapped to attention. 'Cedric Dutton. I called round to see him, managed a good chat about things. He's OK now about you making a home visit, Libby. Just keep it low-key, hmm?'

The practice nurse made a small grimace. 'In other words, don't be a bossy cow.'

Declan grinned. 'I wouldn't have put it quite so bluntly. But he'll respond better if we all gentle him along. He's also agreed to try and socialize a bit. He thought the card morning at the seniors' club might be a start. He'll need transport, though. Ideas, anyone?'

'I'll have a word with Tiny Carruthers,' Moira

said. 'He runs a minibus around to collect the older folk. There are a few with mobility problems. I'm sure he wouldn't mind adding Cedric to his list.'

'*Tiny* Carruthers?' Declan looked a question between the women. 'Is he quite fit himself, then?'

Emma chuckled. 'Perfectly. Tiny is six feet and used to play rugby.'

'I see...' Declan raised an eyebrow.

'He treats the older folk like they're the most important people in the world,' Moira enlarged. 'Cedric will be well looked after.'

'Good.' Declan nodded approval. 'I'll leave that in your capable hands, then, Moira. Now, as you know, I'm invited to the P&C meeting at the school tonight to put our case for the pool to be opened for the seniors' use. I wondered, Moira, whether you'd be free to come with me?'

'Me?' Moira looked flustered. 'What would you need me to do?'

'What you do best.' Declan tipped the older woman a reassuring smile. 'Advocate for the seniors. I can cover the obvious health benefits that participating in physical activity brings. Like helping to strengthen bones and muscles and so reduce the possibility of falls and so on.'

'To say nothing of maintaining folk's independence and social connection,' Moira added, warming to her role. 'And water aerobics is so low-impact and lovely. It's such a shame the pool can't be put to use for the benefit of our older folk.'

'You've convinced me.' Looking pleased, Declan leaned back in his chair and folded his arms.

'Oh, heavens, I fell right into that, didn't I?' Moira looked a bit bemused. 'But I'm happy to do what I can.'

'Would you like me to swing by and give you a lift to the meeting?' Declan asked.

Moira flapped a hand in dismissal. 'You'd have to come in from the cabin and then detour to collect me.'

'Why go home at all after work?' Emma turned to Declan with a sudden idea. 'Stay and have dinner with me and the kids. Then you can leave from here for the meeting.'

He thought about it for one second. 'Thanks. Like me to cook?'

Remembering Friday night when he'd *cooked* for them, Emma felt her body engulfed in heat. But with the children around there'd be none of *that* happening tonight. She didn't know whether to feel glad or sorry. She lifted her gaze to his and for a second their eyes held and they were lost in a hush of silence, a stillness as profound as a mountain top at dawn. 'No need—' Emma blinked, lifting a hand to clutch the unbuttoned collar of her shirt. 'I'll pop a casserole in the slow-cooker at lunch time. If that's all right with you?'

His rather bemused smile began at his lips and moved to his eyes. 'I'll look forward to it. So, Moira—' he snapped back to attention '—I'll collect you and drop you home after the meeting.'

A few more matters regarding the practice were raised and settled.

'You going all right, Jodi?' Declan asked as the meeting broke up and people began standing and clattering their chairs back into place. 'Finding the job OK?'

'I love the work. It's so…interesting.'

'Perhaps you'll rethink your uni course.' Emma laughed. 'Switch to medicine.'

'Don't think so.' Jodi wrinkled her pert nose. 'I love my thoroughbreds too much.'

'I know it's difficult but try to avoid the temptation to scratch,' Emma told her first patient for the day. Shannon Gilmore had recently moved from North Queensland to settle in Bendemere's much cooler climate.

'Pardon me for saying the obvious, Doctor, but you don't have this wretched condition. Some days I could scratch myself to pieces.' The thirty-year-old's bottom lip quivered. 'I don't think the climate here suits me. I wish we'd never had to leave the north. And I don't think it's fair that the wife has to trundle along like so much baggage wherever the husband's job takes him.'

So, they were dealing with much more than her patient's eczema here. Emma's professional instincts sharpened and she prepared for a longer than usual consult. It was obvious Shannon had issues with alienation and resentment and probably sheer loneliness that were all adding to her stress levels and pushing the symptoms of her eczema into overdrive. Her doctor offering half-baked platitudes was not going to help matters. 'It must be difficult when you have your own career to think about,' she commiserated.

'I didn't have a structured career as such. But I had a nice little shop specialising in home décor. And clients willing to pay quite large sums for my expertise. I loved it...'

Emma thought. 'Is there a possibility you could start something like that here?'

Shannon's smile was brittle. 'If I hear that once more, I'll scream. I was living in the *tropics*, selling pieces in beautiful vibrant colours. Here, it's so cold all the time. Who wants to go out and shop? And the days never warm up.'

'Well, they do, actually.' Emma proffered a wry smile. 'But obviously not to the degree you're accustomed to.'

Shannon's shoulders hunched over.

'I understand things seem a bit bleak and insurmountable at the moment,' Emma said gently. 'But if we can't change that immediately, at least let's see what we can do for your eczema, shall we?'

'I didn't mean to come across as so pathetic and needy...' Shannon's little shrug was almost defensive.

Emma decided no follow-up comment was required. Instead, she said, 'First, I think we should consider the type of clothing you're wearing, Shannon. Overheating is a trigger for the eczema to flare up and the skin to start itching.'

'I just can't seem to get warm.' Shannon's fingers plucked at the bulky-knit jumper she was wearing.

'Anything synthetic is probably not a good choice for you at the moment. You'd be better wearing layers of lighter garments so your skin can breathe. Cotton clothing is good. Check out the shops in Toowoomba. You'll find they have a range of wonderful separates. I'm sure you'll find something to suit you. Now, on more practical matters, I imagine you know it's best to avoid soap and detergents?'

Shannon nodded. 'I use a non-perfumed moisturizer and I'm aware of the food allergy factor.'

'And stress,' Emma added gently.

'I guess...'

'You're obviously on the right track with your food.' Emma smiled. 'But you could try increasing your intake of vitamins A, E and C and fish oil supplements can help rebuild the skin. All that will take a little while to kick in so in the meantime I'll give you a script for a steroid cream as a short-term measure. That should get you back on track and don't hesitate to use a cold compress to help things along.'

'Thanks for this.' Shannon took the script and folded it into her bag. 'And for just listening, I guess...'

At the end of the surgery hours Emma popped her head into Declan's room and asked, 'Are you through for the day?'

He looked up from his computer, his eyes softening. 'One more patient to see.' They exchanged a smile. 'I'll come through when I'm done, OK?'

'Fine. Lauren and I are making an apple crumble for dessert.' She fluttered a two-fingered wave. 'See you.'

Declan still had the smile on his face when he scooted his chair back and got to his feet. Rolling back his shoulders, he stretched. He had a few minutes before his last patient for the day was scheduled. He'd never read so much nor spent so much time on the Net than in the past weeks, he thought a bit ruefully. But there were so many areas where he'd had to refresh his knowledge to function effectively as a family practitioner. But he was getting there. Maybe there was hope for him yet.

CHAPTER TEN

DECLAN walked Moira safely to her door and then returned to his car. The meeting had gone well and he was upbeat about how his suggestions had been taken on board by the committee. It was a good outcome for the seniors. Very good.

Suddenly, he wanted to share his news with Emma. And it wasn't that late. She might still be up. He was only a few minutes from Kingsholme. He could cruise by and see whether her lights were on. Decision made, he started the motor and slid away from the kerb.

When he arrived at Kingsholme, Declan could see one solitary light on at the rear of the house. She was probably in the kitchen. Getting out of the car, he followed the path along the side of the building to the back verandah and mounted the steps. He gave a cursory knock and opened the kitchen door, calling gently, 'Emma? It's me.'

'Declan?' She spun round from the stove and frowned uncertainly. 'I didn't expect you.'

'Hi.' Slightly bemused, he stood with his back

to the door and looked at her. She was dressed in polka-dot winter pyjamas, a cuddly dark blue dressing gown and fluffy socks. She looked adorable and he wanted to hold her for ever. 'I wanted to tell you about the meeting.'

She nodded vaguely. 'I've made some hot chocolate. It'll stretch to two.'

'Thanks.' He rubbed his arms briskly, watching as she tipped the hot milk from the saucepan and filled the two mugs. 'It's cold out there.'

Taking their mugs, they sat at the kitchen table. Declan leaned forward eagerly. 'The committee have agreed to the seniors using the pool. They've even gone a step further and suggested having a huge fundraiser to have it heated.'

'Oh, good.'

'And Moira was impressive—in full flight,' he added with a chuckle. 'The committee didn't know what hit them. Even asked what more they could do for the older folk. I hope something comes of it—' He stopped abruptly. Emma was barely listening. Instead, she was gripping her mug like a lifeline and staring fixedly at the opposite wall. 'Hey...' he said gently, touching her arm to bring her out of her trance-like state. 'Are you all right?'

She looked at him blankly. 'Mum's here.'

A frown touched his eyes. 'Is that a problem?'

'It could be. I haven't told her about you. Only that I have a suitable partner for the practice.'

Declan's frown became more pronounced. 'What are you saying, Emma, that you don't want me to meet her?'

'Of course I want you to meet her!' Her gaze fluttered down and she hesitated. 'But when she hears your name—what if she…?'

'Connects the dots? Emma, we can't be held responsible for what our parents did. We don't even know if they did *anything* untoward. Do we?'

'No…' She swallowed heavily and foolish tears blurred her vision. 'I'd hate for her to be hurt, Declan.'

'Because of us and what we mean to each other? Emma, that's ridiculous.' He took her hands in his and gently chafed them. 'You're imagining wild scenarios that have no basis in fact. I'll meet your mum, OK?' he cajoled softly. 'And we'll go from there.'

She nodded mutely.

'Good.' He gave her fingers an approving squeeze. 'Now, drink your nightcap. It'll help you sleep.' Declan looked thoughtful as he lifted his own mug and took several deep mouthfuls of the hot chocolate. 'When did your mother arrive?'

'Just after you'd left for the meeting. She flew up today from Melbourne and hired a car at the

Brisbane airport. She said she wanted to surprise me.'

Well, she'd certainly done that. Declan finished his drink. 'Is she just here for some family time or—'

'No,' Emma cut in and shook her head. 'There's an auction at one of the heritage homes in Toowoomba tomorrow. She's interested in bidding for a couple of paintings for her gallery. But I imagine she won't stay long. She'll want to get back to her business. We didn't have a chance to talk much. She was tired after the drive so she more or less had a shower and went off to bed.'

'I'll come in early, then.' Declan made up his mind. 'That way, I can at least meet her before she heads off about her day.'

Emma resisted the urge to lean closer and rest her head on his shoulder. Just. 'That might be best. I guess…'

'Emma, we can't keep walking on eggshells about this. Let's just take things as they come.'

'I'm sure you're right.' She drummed up her best and brightest smile.

He glanced at his watch. 'I should go and let you get some sleep.'

'And you as well.' She walked with him to the door. 'See you in the morning,' she said.

Declan cupped her face with both hands. 'I'll be here *early*.'

She gave a nod of understanding and agreement.

'It'll be all right, Emma.' His mouth brushed against hers. 'Trust me.'

The following morning, Emma felt the nerves in her stomach churning endlessly. She'd fed the children and now they'd gone to get dressed for school while she organized their lunches. Earlier, she'd heard her mother's alarm so she'd probably be up and dressed by now... Was Declan on his way in from the cabin? Oh, Lord...

'Morning, darling.'

'Oh—hi, Mum.' Emma's heart rate quickened as her mother came into the kitchen. 'Sleep all right?'

'Seemed a bit odd to be back in Andrew's and my old bedroom. But I slept well. I like the makeover, by the way.'

'It seemed time.' Emma was guarded. 'Now, what about some breakfast?'

'Just toast, thanks. Do you have leaf green tea?'

'China canister there on the shelf. Help yourself. I'll just finish packing the kids' lunches.' Emma's mouth flicked into a quick smile. 'You look lovely, by the way.' Dressed in her beautifully tailored black trousers and jacket, her mother looked Melbourne *chic* all the way. 'Your boots are *gorgeous.*'

'And comfortable. I expect to be doing a bit of running around today.'

Emma watched as her mother slid bread into the toaster. 'Are you after anything else beside the paintings?'

'The Kingsley estate was vast. There are some extremely delicate tapestries I might go after—if the price is right,' she added with a wry smile.

True to his word, Declan arrived early at Kingsholme. He unloaded his medical case in his consulting room and then made his way through to the living quarters. He heard muted conversation from the vicinity of the kitchen and guessed the voices belonged to Emma and her mother. His heart did a quick tango. He'd pretended to be calm about things for Emma's sake. But he was far from it. Mrs Armitage's reaction could ruin everything he and Emma had found. He hoped with all that was in him it wouldn't come to that.

Reaching the kitchen, he paused and then leant against the doorframe and poked his head in. Emma's mother was standing against the bench of cupboards, a delicate teacup in her hands. At least he supposed it was her mother. She looked like an older version of her daughter. Declan's gaze flicked discreetly and quickly over the slender-framed woman. She oozed style and sophistication in her dress and *very* good gold jewellery decorated her throat and hands. Hell, he hoped he'd measure up. He cleared his throat. 'Good morning.'

'Declan!' Her heart thumping, Emma turned, holding Lauren's lunch box like a shield against her chest. 'Come in. Um—this is my mother. Mum—' she smiled, her voice a bit breathless, earnest with her own need for things to go well '—this is Declan O'Malley, my practice partner.'

Emma's mother turned with a graceful movement and replaced her cup on its saucer and then held out her hand. 'Declan. How very nice to meet you.'

'Mrs Armitage.' Declan's handshake was firm. 'It's good to meet you too.'

'Oh, please. Call me Roz.' The older woman smiled. 'You've an early start this morning?'

'Most mornings,' Declan replied. 'But we don't mind, do we, Emma?' His wide-open gaze seemed natural and frank but it was telling Emma so much more. First hurdle over. It will be all right.

'It's like most jobs, I guess,' Emma said, getting

into the spirit of the conversation. 'You get into a rhythm of sorts.'

Declan looked hopefully around the kitchen. 'Any tea going, guys?'

'I've just made a pot if you like green tea?' Roz offered.

'Sounds just the ticket,' Declan said diplomatically, even though he would have preferred Emma's strong brew first thing. As he poured himself a cup, he set out to be sociable. 'Emma tells me you have a busy day ahead, Roz.'

'Yes, and I should get going.' Emma's mother glanced at her watch. 'The paintings I want to bid for are up first thing. I shouldn't be too late home, though, darling,' she told Emma. 'Penny and Clive Bailleau are driving in from Munbilla and we're meeting up for lunch. After that, I'm pretty much done.'

'Oh, I'm glad you're seeing friends,' Emma said warmly. 'Give Penny and Clive my best.'

'I'll do that.' Roz rinsed her cup and placed it in the drainer. Turning, she plucked a section of paper towel and dried her hands. 'And I thought I might pick up a treat for the children,' she said in a confidential undertone. 'What are they into?'

'Oh, that's so nice of you, Mum.' Emma's heart warmed.

Roz flapped a hand in dismissal. 'They've had

a hard time, from what you said. And I'd like to do it anyway.'

'OK—' Emma thought for a second. 'Well, Lauren likes to read and she's keen to learn to ride, although she knows practically nothing about horses. Not sure about Joel…'

'He's mad about soccer,' Declan chimed in with a grin. 'At the moment, he's kicking a clapped-out piece of leather around the yard. I had it on my list to get him a decent soccer ball but now I'll leave it in your capable hands, Roz.'

'So—' Roz Armitage held up two crossed fingers '—the book shop and the sports shop, right? Now, I really must be on my way.'

'Take care on the roads.' Emma gave her mother a quick hug.

'And you two have a good day,' Roz said in reply and wrinkled her nose. 'If that's possible.'

'It is, Roz,' Declan quirked his mouth and drawled, 'even in medicine.'

Two hours later, Declan realized the rashness of that statement.

They had an emergency situation at the hospital. Students from a girls' school in Toowoomba were being brought in with suspected food poisoning. 'Apparently they're here in Bendemere on a school camp,' Moira told the doctors as they came together for a quick briefing. 'Both our ambulances have gone out and the teachers will bring the rest in the school bus.'

'The rest!' Declan's head pulled back. 'How many are we expecting?'

'Maybe in excess of ten?' Moira made a small grimace. 'They're from the upper grades, thirteen and upwards.'

'So at least we can expect some degree of cooperation and sensible answers,' he commented ruefully.

'Nursing backup might be a bit thin on the ground at the hospital,' Emma said. 'No doubt Rachel will call in casuals but apparently a few of the regular nurses are off with winter ills. Perhaps Libby could fill in and come with us?'

Declan nodded. 'Good idea. And Moira, do what you have to do to reorganize our patient list, please.'

'Anyone who is just waiting for repeats of their scripts could perhaps come back tomorrow,' Emma added. 'Whatever, we'll leave things in your capable hands.'

'Do we have any idea of the expected ETA?' Declan asked as they pulled in to the hospital car park.

'They won't be long,' Emma said. 'Camp Kookaburra is only about ten kilometres out.'

From the back seat of the car, Libby pondered, 'I wonder what they ate?'

Declan snorted. 'Something dodgy for breakfast, if they've all gone down so quickly.'

Within minutes the ambulances arrived, followed by the school bus.

Emma could see at once that the students were quite ill, some of them pale and sweaty. They were going to take some sorting out, that was certain.

Declan grimaced. 'Bang goes the rest of our morning surgery list.'

'Rural doctoring,' Emma reminded him.

'Got it.' Declan lifted a finger, acknowledging her point.

Talitha looked goggle-eyed at the volume of patients. 'We'll run out of cubicles! Where will we put them all?'

'We'll put some of them out on the verandah ward.' Rachel was in full flight in charge. 'And Tally, run and get bags or basins, please. They're bound to be still vomiting.'

Tally ran.

'Right, guys,' Declan came in authoritatively, 'Let's get some triage going, shall we?'

'Sorry I'm late.' Casual nurse Irene McCosker,

fiftyish, arrived slightly breathless, still adjusting the belt on her uniform trousers. 'Jeff's off sick so I had to shoo the customers out and close the shop,' she explained.

Emma smiled at the older woman. 'Thanks so much for coming in at short notice, Irene. Perhaps, where you can, would you start taking names, please? And liaise with the accompanying teachers about letting the parents know. That would be a great help.'

'Certainly, Dr Armitage.' Irene looked pleased to be given responsibility.

'We should see the kids on stretchers first,' Emma said quietly to Declan. 'Would you like to team with Rachel? Then Libby and I can work together.'

His brow furrowed for a second. 'If you're sure?'

She nodded. 'Absolutely.' He'd said it was all about trust and so far he hadn't let her down.

Accompanied by Rachel, Declan went into the first cubicle. Their patient looked pale and clammy. Bending over the stretcher, Declan asked, 'What's your name, sweetheart?'

'Bronte Pearce.'

'And how old are you, Bronte?'

'Sixteen.'

'And when did you start feeling ill?'

'Soon after breakfast—' The youngster rocked her head restlessly from side to side and moaned softly.

'It'll be all right, honey.' Rachel smoothed the girl's long dark fringe away from her forehead. 'We'll get you feeling better soon.'

'Bronte,' Declan came in gently, 'I just need to feel your tummy.' His mouth compressed as he palpated. 'Right.' He stepped back and drew the sheet up. 'That's fine. Have you had any diarrhoea?'

'Some. Oh—help…' Her plea came out on a moan.

Noticing her patient's sudden pallor, Rachel reached for a basin and helped her sit up. Then, exhausted from the bout of vomiting, Bronte fell back on the pillows. She blocked a tear with the palm of her hand. 'I feel awful,' she sniffed. 'And my little sister Sasha is so ill. She's only thirteen and she started her periods just yesterday…'

'It's OK, sweetie. Don't worry.' Rachel squeezed Bronte's hand. 'She'll be well looked after.'

'Someone's head should roll for this.' Grim-faced, Declan scribbled instructions on the chart. 'Put up ten milligrams of maxolon stat, please, Rachel. That should settle her tummy.'

'Lomotil for the diarrhoea?'

Declan nodded. 'Let's start with two orally and

cut back to one after each bowel movement.' He frowned. 'She's dehydrating. I'd like her on four per cent glucose and one-fifth normal saline IV. Sips of water only. Could you take her blood sugar levels as well, please? Anything below three, I need to know. And, while you're doing that,' he added, replacing the chart, 'I'll just have a quick word with Emma.'

Declan found Emma in the next cubicle and beckoned her aside. 'Have you treated a child by the name of Sasha Pearce yet?'

'I've just sent her to the ward,' Emma confirmed. 'She was seriously dehydrated. She'll need to stay on a drip for some time yet. I'm recommending we keep her overnight.'

'How was she generally?'

'As you'd expect—scared and miserable. Is there a problem?' Emma queried.

'I've just seen her older sister, Bronte. She was concerned.'

And so are you, Emma decided. Declan really cared about these kids and that thought warmed her through and through. 'Tally's taken Sasha under her wing, Declan. Trust me, she'll be fine.'

'OK, thanks. I'll just relay that to Bronte.' He hesitated. 'Poor kid was pretty upset about her little sister's predicament.'

'The women's business?' Emma shot him a look as old as time. 'All taken care of.'

'Great. Thanks.' He swished back the curtains and disappeared.

They went on assessing and treating their juvenile patients for the next couple of hours, answering questions from anxious parents as they trickled in to check on their offspring. Several of the students appeared quite poorly and had to be admitted for observation but the majority were treated and allowed to go home.

'Did you get any joy from the Health Department?' Emma asked later, as they made their way out of the hospital to the car park.

'They've promised urgent action,' Declan said. 'Obviously, whatever they find will be sent for analysis. In the meantime, the camp has been cut short. Most of the kids will be home in their own beds by tonight.'

Moira had refused to overload the lists so the afternoon surgery finished in reasonable time. After his last patient had left, Declan went along to Emma's consulting room. He knocked and poked his head in. 'All done for the day?'

'Mmm.' She waved him in and swung off her chair as if her feet had wings. 'Hi...' She met his gaze, an almost shy smile playing over her lips. And Declan knew he'd crack wide open if he didn't kiss her.

He held out his arms and she flew into them, wrapping herself tightly around him and turning her face up for his kiss.

'Emma...' A gravelly sigh dragged itself up from the depths of his chest and his mouth took hers as if he were dying of thirst.

She shifted against him, each tiny movement a subtle invitation for him to hold her more tightly, more intimately.

And he did.

Heat exploded in him and he gave a strangled groan, her soft pleas driving him closer to the edge. For a split second he considered letting his natural instincts run wild and making love with her here in her office. To be inside her, to feel her legs wrapped round him, hear the sweet sounds of her climax...

But only for a second. Suddenly, the compulsion took flight. Somehow it seemed tacky and not worthy of her—of them.

But how he ached for her.

He found just enough control to break the kiss. 'Emma...' He pressed his forehead to hers. 'We have to slow down.'

'Yes, I know...' Her voice shook. 'But I wish—'

'Wish we didn't?' He gave a hard laugh. 'Opportunities are a bit unworkable at the moment.' He released her, then slid his hands down her arms to mesh her fingers with his. 'Our time will come,' he promised huskily.

'I suppose…yes.' She hung her head a little. 'Can you at least stay for dinner?'

'Nice thought, but no.' He leaned forward, brushing her mouth with his lips. 'You should have some quality time with your mother. Somehow, I think it's what you both need.'

She smiled unwillingly. 'Guru is your middle name now, is it?'

'Christopher, actually.' They looked at each other for a long moment and suddenly her eyes clouded. Declan shook his head. 'You're not still worrying about all that stuff regarding our respective parents, are you, Emma?'

'Perhaps a bit.'

He frowned. 'Why, for crying out loud? Roz was clearly very at ease when I met her.'

'I wonder—' Emma bit her lips together and hesitated. 'I mean—I hope Dad didn't deceive her. That would be too awful.'

'Emma, Emma.' Declan pulled her in close again, his patience clearly under strain. 'For your own sake, you have to let this go. None of it matters now. You do see that, don't you?'

'Yes, you're right. None of it matters.' Well, one part of her believed that. The logical, clear-thinking part. But underneath there was still a tiny doubt, niggling away like a bothersome pebble in a shoe.

But clearly Declan wanted to close the page, to put the discussion to rest once and for all. Deep down, she knew it was the best option. And yet… 'You're right,' she said again, as if she really meant it. 'None of it matters now.'

'Tell me again how you and Dad met.'

The children had long gone to bed and Emma and Roz, both dressed in their nightwear, were sitting in front of the fire. 'Darling, I've already told you several times, as I recall,' Roz said mildly.

'But not since I was about fourteen.' Emma filled their tiny glasses with a peach-flavoured liqueur. 'Now Dad's gone, it would be nice to hear it again,' Emma pleaded. 'And from the beginning, please.'

Roz gave a resigned kind of smile. 'We were both at Uni. I was doing fine arts. Andrew was doing medicine. I guess it was unlikely we would meet up at all, both doing very different disciplines. But there was a move on to close the crèche at the university.'

'Why?' Emma asked, more than a little interested.

'Oh, someone in a high place got a bee in his bonnet that babies and young children had no business being on campus.' Roz lifted a shoulder. 'Independently, both Andrew and I had read the flyers that were asking for numbers to rally to protest against the decision. And we both went along.'

'So you met waving banners.' Emma smiled, her chin parked on her upturned hand.

'Something like that.' Roz took a sip of her liqueur. 'As I remember, we were pretty outraged. We linked up and formed a committee and in time the idea to close the crèche was vetoed. In those days, most of the students who used the crèche were single mums. They really needed the facility.'

'So, you and Dad must have had very strong feelings about child welfare,' Emma pressed.

'We did.' Roz nodded her ash-blonde head. 'In fact, when the director at the crèche called for volunteers occasionally, we both went and helped out with the little ones. We both loved kids,' she added quietly.

'And yet you only had me.'

Roz responded to the question in her daughter's eyes with a tiny shrug of her shoulders. 'I didn't enjoy being pregnant,' she confessed. 'Andrew understood. But we delighted in you when you were born, Emma. So much.' She frowned a bit. 'You never felt...*unloved*, did you?'

'No, of course not.' Even as she said the words Emma felt the painful lurch in her heart. But, knowing what she did now, had that been the reason her father had drifted towards Anne O'Malley? A young widow with her little brood? He must have felt so *needed*. Would it be going too far to say even *fulfilled*? She swallowed deeply. 'Were you and Dad always happy together?'

'Yes, we were.' There was no hesitation in Roz's reply. 'It wasn't easy being married to a doctor, Emma. It took me a long time to realize the demands of Andrew's job. His patients always came first. I thought he was busy enough when he was at the Prince Alfred, but then, when he was offered tenure at John Bosco's, he got even busier. He was always very involved with his interns.' Roz gave a faintly wry smile. 'I guess in a way they became like his own kids.'

They were quiet for a while and then Emma said carefully, 'I sometimes wondered why you went off to Melbourne to open your gallery and left Dad here.'

'Yes...I suppose you did.' Roz sighed, slightly daunted by the need for explanation. 'Your dad thoroughly approved, you know, Emma. In fact, he suggested it. I'd put my own career on hold when we came here to Kingsholme. But I knew how much it meant to your father.'

'You never really settled here, though, did you?'

Roz laughed shortly. 'And I thought I hid it so well. It was different, that's all. I made a life, formed a few good friendships. I was managing. But suddenly, out of the blue, Andrew suggested the gallery idea. You'd returned to the practice. Dad was quite sure you'd found your niche in rural medicine. And he was so proud to have you as his practice partner.'

'Yes, he told me that.' Emma looked down at her hands. 'But he missed *you*, Mum.'

'We missed one another,' Roz said patiently. 'But all along he'd planned to join me in Melbourne as soon as he'd found someone to replace him at Kingsholme. Someone he was sure would work well with you. Someone he could trust. He wanted to have it all lined up before he told you. Unfortunately, it didn't work out quite like that...'

'No...' Tears blurred Emma's vision and she reached for her mother's hand.

They stayed like that for some minutes more, both with a new sense of calm and acceptance.

'We should have talked like this a long time ago,' Emma said.

'My fault.' Roz looked a little sad. 'I had to grieve for Andrew on my own. He meant the world to me…'

Emma searched her mother's face. 'We should have grieved together.'

'Yes, I see that now. I do love you, darling.'

The reassurance flooded into Emma like warm sunshine parting a cloudy sky. 'I love you too, Mum.'

'Mum's under the impression Dad was still looking for a suitable practice partner for me when he died,' Emma told Declan the next day. They were sitting over a cuppa after surgery had finished.

'Maybe that's for the best,' Declan said. 'But *we* know Andrew tried his best to make sure both your and Roz's futures were assured when he was out of the picture.'

Emma gave a tiny shrug. 'Yes.'

Declan's jaw worked for a minute. 'If only I'd been able to fly out at the time Andrew first called me, instead of being banged up in a hospital rehab unit—'

'But you did come, Declan. You came as soon as you could. And Dad's wishes were fulfilled.'

'Did Roz get home all right?' he asked, changing the tenor of the conversation subtly.

'Yes. She rang about an hour ago. And you were right.' Emma felt a mix of emotions tumble around inside her. 'Mum and I did need to talk.' She stopped and bit down on her bottom lip. 'I think I've matched up all the pieces now.' And, if there was one small piece that still refused to go exactly where she wanted it to, well, so be it.

He smiled. 'I'm glad. By the way, I had some other news today about the Jones family. Carolyn has gone on holiday and Adam was discharged from hospital. For the present, he's staying with Tracey at the shelter.'

'Well, I guess that's progress of a sort.'

'I think we can assume that.' Declan moved restively in his chair. 'Just means you'll have Lauren and Joel for a bit longer, I guess.' And longer still until they could make love again...

CHAPTER ELEVEN

A WEEK later and the staff were on their lunch break before the afternoon clinic.

'Bendemere is hosting the schools' annual sports day tomorrow,' Emma said.

Declan looked up from his reading. 'Is it a big event?'

'All the schools from the neighbouring districts compete.' Jodi dipped into her mug of soup. 'It's a big deal. I was sports captain both years Bendemere won,' she added modestly.

'So, you want the day off tomorrow to go strut your stuff, do you?' Declan teased.

Jodi wrinkled her nose at him. 'I work at the supermarket tomorrow,' she reminded him.

'Lauren's race isn't until eleven.' Emma gave a tentative look around the faces. 'And, as she doesn't have her mum to cheer her on, I thought I might try to get across to the sports ground.'

'I'll cover your list,' Declan offered promptly. 'In fact, I might try to get along for Lauren's race myself. How are tomorrow's lists looking, Moira?'

'Fairly light,' Moira said. 'Most folk will be at the sports day.'

Declan lifted a hand and rubbed the back of his neck. 'Nev can't make it?'

'My guess is he would have used up all his family leave,' Moira said. 'I doubt he'd want to ask for a day off to go to his grandchildren's sports day.'

Emma looked at Declan. 'So, it's agreed I'll go?'

'No question.' Declan leaned back in his chair and folded his arms. 'What about Joel's events?'

'He's involved only in team events. I think he's more concerned about the food on the day,' Emma ended with a chuckle. Then she sobered. 'But I think it would make Lauren feel special if I was there for her.'

'Yes, it would,' Declan said softly. He wanted to lean forward and kiss her on the lips and tell her what a great job she was doing as a stand-in parent. Instead, he restrained himself and went back to his reading.

At a few minutes to eleven the next day, Emma took her place among the parents and supporters who were rapidly filling every space along the sides of the running track.

'Which one is your kiddie?' a friendly lady who looked like someone's nanna asked as she made room for Emma beside her.

'Over there.' Emma smiled, pointing to Lauren, her little face fierce in concentration as the children began to line up. 'Her mum can't be here so I'm standing in,' she felt compelled to add.

'That's my granddaughter, Taylor, beside her,' the older woman said.

She's at least a head taller than Lauren, Emma thought, her heart dropping. She'd been hoping like mad for Lauren to win. Even a small victory like winning a race would be magic for the child.

Emma felt strung tight, waiting for the starter's whistle to sound. So focused was she that it was a moment before she registered the tap on her shoulder. Spinning round, she took a quick breath of surprise. 'Declan! How did you manage to get here?'

'Easy.' He grinned. 'I booted the patients out of the waiting room and told them to come back tomorrow.'

Emma rolled her eyes.

'Moira and I juggled things. Several agreed to an after-hours consult. I'll see them.' Moving closer, he rested his hand on Emma's shoulder. 'Am I here in time for Lauren's race?'

'They're lining up now.' Emma flicked a hand. 'Lauren seems like a little sprite next to some of the others.'

'I bet you she's a pint-size rocket.' Declan increased the pressure on his hold. 'Look! They're off!' he yelled. 'Go, Lauren!'

The race, it seemed, took only seconds—seconds when they cheered themselves hoarse. Running like the wind, pace for pace with her rival, Lauren finally pulled out a burst of speed from somewhere within her slender little body and took the lead, sprinting over the finishing line just centimetres in front of her rival.

'She won! Lauren won!' Unable to contain her excitement, Emma grabbed at Declan and he whirled her around until she was breathless.

'Come on—' He grabbed her hand and together they began moving towards the finish line.

'Lauren!' Emma shrieked. 'Honey, over here!'

'Wait—' Declan hauled Emma to a halt beside him. 'Look...' he said with something like disbelief in his voice.

Emma looked. 'Oh, my goodness,' she whispered and took a shaky breath. 'It's Tracey... Oh, Declan!' she exclaimed softly. 'Lauren's wish has come true. She so wanted Tracey to be here to watch her run.'

'Lauren's got her mum back,' he rejoined quietly, and their eyes linked in understanding.

Together they watched as Lauren threw herself into her mother's arms. It was the hug of a lifetime. A hug that went on and on, mother and child clinging together and looking as though they never wanted to be parted ever again.

Declan squeezed Emma's hand. 'Are we going over to say hello?'

'Maybe we should. Unless…do you think we'd be intruding?'

'No, I don't,' Declan said and he smiled. 'Come on.'

Lauren's little face lit up when she saw Emma. 'I won!' she said and her thousand-watt smile said it all.

'You did.' Emma held out her arms. 'Well done, sweetheart. You ran like the wind.'

Lauren allowed Emma a brief fierce hug and then she slipped back to her mother's side, tucking her skinny little arm through Tracey's very possessively.

Emma felt something crack inside her. Was it a feeling of loss? she wondered. But that was silly. She was never going to have Lauren indefinitely. She was back with her mother now and that was how it should be. But how she was going to miss that sweet child.

'Hello, Tracey.' Declan stuck out his hand. 'This is a real turn-up.' He grinned. 'You look great, by the way.'

'Thanks.' Tracey looked shyly between the two doctors. 'Marcella from the shelter drove me over. She's got Adam with her.'

'That's wonderful,' Emma said warmly. 'I'm so glad you managed to get here.'

Tracey held her daughter's hand tightly. 'I wouldn't have missed it. I would have got here somehow.'

'Are you back home with us now, Mum?' Lauren's big brown eyes asked the question neither Declan nor Emma had felt able to.

'Yes, baby, I am,' Tracey said softly and bent to press a kiss on her daughter's fair head. 'We'll all be back at Granddad's tonight.'

'You're going to miss them.' Practical as always, Moira was helping Emma pack up the children's clothes for their return home.

Emma blinked a bit, popping a pair of Lauren's jeans into the suitcase. 'Their place is with their mother now she's well. I was just the stopgap until things got back to normal.'

Moira kept folding. 'This house was made for children.'

'And maybe one day it will have some here permanently.' Ignoring Moira's not too subtle implication, Emma forced lightness into her voice. Already a gnawing kind of emptiness was beginning to surround her. But she'd get over it. She had to. 'Oh, Moira—hang on a tick before you close the case. I've something for Lauren. I'll just get it.' She came back with a jumper in the softest, purest wool. It was a happy poppy-red colour with a chain of daisies embroidered around the neckline.

'That's...lovely,' Moira said, but with a note of disquiet in her voice. 'But Emma, should you be spending so much money on the child?'

'It's a gift, nothing more, nothing less.' Emma folded the jumper neatly between some layers of tissue paper and placed it on top of the rest of the clothes. 'I thought Lauren might like to wear it when she goes riding. I want her to keep up her lessons.'

Moira sniffed. 'And who's paying for those riding lessons? You?'

Emma replaced the lid of the suitcase and zipped it shut. 'With respect, Moira, that's my business. Jodi and I have come to an arrangement.'

'You're just like your father.' Moira shook her

head. 'Your heart overrules common sense some-times. Let's just hope Tracey doesn't mess things up for those children again,' she added darkly.

'She won't.' Emma was firm. 'People have worked very hard with her and she's responded. For once, it's been a good outcome.'

'You're going to be at a loose end tonight.' It was late on the same day and Declan was grabbing a coffee before heading out to a house call.

'I suppose I will.' Emma looked up from giving the kitchen bench a quick tidy. 'Got any solutions?'

'I might.' Placing his mug carefully back on the counter top, he half turned to look at her. 'Come home with me.'

There was a moment's loaded silence. Emma blinked uncertainly and she realized what he was saying. She'd been thinking only about the children's departure and how it would affect her. She'd completely forgotten that, with their going, her life was her own again. Her options were suddenly wide open. 'I hadn't thought—'

'Well, I have.' He looked at his watch. 'I'm about to do this house call, then I'll see the three after-hours patients. Should be through by six-thirty. Put a few things together, hmm? And something for work tomorrow.'

'All right.' She smiled, swallowing back a throatful of emotions. 'I'll be ready.'

She hadn't been in his bedroom before.

It was almost spartan with a king-sized bed, books on the bedside table, family photos in a fold-out frame, a set of weights in the corner. And why was she even noticing?

Declan put her bag on the end table. 'Do you want to hang anything?'

'Um—yes, please.' Emma slipped past him to hang her work clothes in the wardrobe. She tried to swallow. Her mouth had become so dry and her heart, with a mind of its own, had gravitated to her throat. It seemed ages since they'd been lovers. Perhaps she'd imagined more than the reality. Could they possibly recapture what they'd found together? And, if they couldn't— what then?

'Emma...'

'Declan, what if...?'

He shook his head, drawing her down to sit on the edge of the bed. He stared at her for a moment. Then, lifting his hands, he cupped her face. 'Emma, do you trust me?'

The catch in his voice told her everything she needed to hear. 'Yes.'

* * *

'Oh, heavens! Look at the time!' Emma sprang upright and then leaned down to tug Declan awake. 'Declan, get up! We've only minutes to get to the surgery!'

He groaned. 'What's the hurry? They can't start without us.'

'But it'll look odd if we straggle in late. *And together.*'

'As if we care.' He reached up and pulled her back under the covers. 'I want to tell the world we're together.'

'Oh...' Emma felt her lips sigh apart. 'Really?'

He pulled her closer, nuzzling her throat, behind her ear, then her throat again. 'Yes, really. What about you, Emma? Want to shout it to the tree tops?'

'It's all so new,' she offered, hardly knowing what her answer should be but tucking further into his closeness. His body felt deliciously warm, hard, expectant. Wonderful. All for her. 'Yes, oh, yes,' she said at last and turned her face to meet his mouth.

They tasted each other, taking it slowly, each press of their lips renewing their sense of wonder and delight. Emma closed her eyes and let it happen, letting her tongue tease him and her breath sigh over his face. She ran her hands along his torso, up the lightly tanned curve of his neck and into the dark, soft strands of his hair.

And she didn't let herself think for one second that this commitment was anything but right. Right and perfect.

She opened her mouth wider on his, letting herself drown in his kiss, flinging her doubts into the air like a handful of sand in the wind.

Emma drifted through the morning surgery in a cocoon of dreamy recollection as memories of their lovemaking rolled over her. She felt as though someone had poured liquid sunshine over her bones. She was in love. In love with the most wonderful man in the world.

When, only seconds later, Declan rapped on the door and stuck his head in, she started up out of her reverie, snapping back to reality when he said starkly, 'We have the worst kind of emergency, Emma. Jodi's had a fall at the stables. It looks bad.'

'Oh, my God!' Emma's hand went to her mouth. 'How bad?'

He shook his head. 'Let's get out there. Every second counts.'

Declan looked strained as he took the emergency kit from Libby. 'Keep the hospital in the loop, please, Libs.' The nurse merely nodded.

Moira hovered, her face pale with shock. 'I know you want to come with us, Moira,' Declan said gently. 'But—'

'I'd be in the way.' Her mouth trembled. 'Take care of her, Declan. She's the dearest thing on earth to me.'

Emma wrapped an arm quickly around Moira's shoulders. 'We'll let you know the minute we have some details,' she promised.

'Do you have any more details about the accident?' Emma asked.

'Not much. Jodi was riding track with several others. Apparently, the horses were flat out in a time trial. The lead horse stumbled. Jodi was immediately behind.'

Emma sucked in her breath on a grimace. It would be a domino effect, resulting in a wild mix of riders, horses, limbs and bodies.

'Jodi's parents?' Declan's question took on the practicalities of the situation.

'Last I heard, they're away on holiday up north somewhere. She was staying with Moira.'

'Siblings?'

'One brother at Uni in Brisbane. Final year engineering.' Worst scenarios curled in a knot in Emma's stomach. Jodi's family would have to be summoned immediately.

When they arrived at the stables, they were out

of the car and running. Jodi's cries of distress were endless. Heartbreaking. Emma ran faster.

Sarah McGinty was waiting. 'I tried to make her more comfortable,' she said. 'But I didn't dare move her. Patrick and James are away at the yearling sales. There's just me here.' She tightened her arms across her middle as if she was in pain herself. 'None of this should have happened…'

Emma placed a quick hand of sympathy on Sarah's forearm and squeezed.

The doctors worked seamlessly as a team, checking first for any head or spinal injury. 'Stay with us, Jodi,' Declan said gently. He slipped the oxygen mask into place. 'We'll have you feeling better soon.'

And pigs might fly, he added silently, grimly.

Emma was doing her best to insert an IV. She shook her head.

'Problem?' Declan snapped.

'Veins thready and constricted. OK,' she said with relief. 'I've got it. Normal saline going in now. What pain relief do you want?'

'Spleen seems OK. We can give morphine. Let's make it five milligrams, please. Anti-emetic ten. Both IV.'

'Jodi, sweetheart, we're giving you something for the pain now.' Emma injected the drugs quickly. 'All done.'

'Thanks. I need to assess what's going on with her legs.'

Emma knew what had to be done. Grabbing the scissors from the emergency pack, she slit Jodi's jodhpurs from ankle to thigh, peeling back the layers of material. She bit hard on her bottom lip at what lay revealed. Bone was protruding from Jodi's thigh.

'Compound fracture to the right femur.' Declan was clinically calm. 'I'd guess the horse in its fright has kicked out and caught her legs.' His fingers ran gently along her shins. 'Multiple fractures to left tib and fib so both legs compromised. Let's get a doughnut dressing over that exposed bone, please, and we'll splint both legs together for the transfer to the ambulance.'

'For the best possible care, I think we should chopper her straight through to the Royal Brisbane.' Emma's tone was unequivocal. 'She's going to need hours of surgery and follow-up rehab.' She drew out her mobile phone. 'I'll put a call into CareFlight. Ask them to meet us at the hospital. By the time they get here, we should have Jodi stable enough to go.'

Two of the town's ambulance crew who had arrived barely minutes behind the doctors moved in with the stretcher. Nick Turner, the senior officer, looked stricken. 'I've known young Jodi all her life...'

Declan's mouth drew in. This was no time to start handwringing. Their patient needed to be in the care of a surgeon and fast. 'What's the situation with the other riders, Nick?'

'There were two lads. Both managed to roll out of the way of the horses. They're a bit shaken. No obvious injuries and we've checked their neuro obs.' He shook his head. 'Poor little Jodi was caught in the middle of the scrum. Blasted animals...'

Emma closed off her mobile. 'The base can't give us an ETA on the chopper. It's presently evacuating injured from a motor pile-up on the Warrego Highway.'

Declan's expletive was muted. 'What now?'

Emma bit her lips together. Declan's face spoke volumes.

'We could take her by ambulance to Toowoomba and try and get backup transport from there,' Nick said without much conviction. 'The road's still a bit dodgy in places from the storm but if we're careful...'

Declan shook his head. 'We can't put Jodi through that.'

'Then we'll wait on the chopper,' Emma said doggedly.

Declan's jaw tightened. God only knew what Jodi's circulation would be doing by the time the air ambulance got to them. And they were wasting precious seconds messing about here. Jodi's cry of distress sent a chill around the gathering.

'I'll check again with CareFlight.' Emma pulled out her mobile.

'Hold it,' Declan said clearly. 'I'll do the surgery here.'

Emma's eyes flew wide in alarm. Did Declan realize what he was suggesting? Surely he was placing their patient's life at risk if he didn't know for certain whether he had the stamina to complete the operation? Should she try to intervene and stop him? 'Declan—'

In an abrupt movement, he drew her aside. 'I need you to back me on this, Emma. It'll be a far better outcome for Jodi if she can have the surgery done here.'

But would it be the best outcome for *him*? Operating before he was ready could undo all the progress, both physically and emotionally, that he'd made. And she knew if she dug her toes in and refused to back him, he'd respect their professional partnership and stand aside and wait for the chopper. But what of Jodi? Poor little injured Jodi. The wait would be terrible. For all of them.

'Emma, listen…' he said, his jaw working. 'I can do this.'

Emma closed her eyes, praying for courage, because this was the hardest decision she'd ever had to make in her life. Her heart pounded. She thought of her father and what he'd want her to do. He'd tell her to trust her instincts. She closed her eyes for one second and then snapped them open. 'As long as you're sure, I'll back you.'

'Thank you.' Declan already had his mobile phone in his hand. He punched a logged-in number and waited to be connected. 'Rachel? Declan. We're still at the stables. The chopper's a no-show. We're bringing Jodi in now. I'll do the surgery. I'll have to pin and plate so I'll need all orthopaedic trays sterilized and ready.'

'Word of the RTA is all over the TV news,' Rachel said. 'I've gone ahead and anticipated your request.'

'Brilliant—thanks.' Declan felt a huge weight begin to slide from his shoulders. They could do this. 'What nursing backup can we manage?'

'Well, I'll scrub, of course, and I've got Dot here. She's theatre-savvy, even if she doesn't get much practice these days.'

'Oliver Shackelton lined up to gas for us?'

'There we might have a slight problem.' Rachel

sounded cautious. 'I called Oliver. He's had flu, and he's feeling too rocky to be in Theatre.'

'So, we don't have an anaesthetist?' Declan just resisted thumping his fist against his forehead in frustration. What options did he have now to safely go ahead with Jodi's surgery? 'Just give me a second here, Rachel.'

Beside him, Emma got the gist of the conversation and wondered what unkind fate had singled her out today. She felt as though her professional integrity had been pushed to the limits. It wasn't fair. Emotion, real and powerful, churned inside her. Could she take this last step that would enable Declan to operate? Could she afford not to? When did it become obligation to speak up? Was it safer to just stand aside and wait?

In her heart, she knew the decision had already been made for her.

'Declan?'

Her fleeting touch in the small of his back had his gaze swivelling in her direction. He shrugged. 'Looks like we're stuffed,' he said flatly. 'Oliver can't help.'

'But perhaps I can.' She looked unflinchingly at him. 'I did my elective in anaesthesiology. I could probably manage. But it will be a long op. I'll need Oliver's input on dosage for longer-acting drugs.

But if you think the whole thing's too risky, I want you to pull out now.'

Declan shook his head. In his mind there were no doubts left and only three words to be said. 'We'll go ahead.'

Emma could hardly believe how smoothly their little hospital was coping with the emergency. She was still basking in a sense of pride as she finished scrubbing. The sound of a door swishing open sent her turning away from the basin and, by the time Declan had begun scrubbing beside her, she was drying her hands and asking sharply, 'You OK?'

'Yep.' He sent her an abrupt look from under his brows and grinned. 'Glad I had that extra X-ray equipment installed, though.'

'Even though we'll be paying for it for the rest of our lives.'

'Oh, tut, Emma. We've managed so far, haven't we?'

She had to admit they had. And she knew they were batting light conversation around because to get too serious now would be more than either of them could cope with. The decision to operate here had been made. They just had to make sure they gave it their all.

'See you in there.' She turned and left the annexe and crossed to the theatre. Rachel had prepared the anaesthetic trolley perfectly and Emma felt a rush of adrenalin she hadn't experienced for the longest time.

She'd do a brilliant job for Jodi.

They all would.

The surgery took almost seven hours. Hours when Emma felt her skills were being tested mercilessly. Even though the monitors indicated Jodi was handling the anaesthetic well, Emma knew she couldn't afford to relax her vigilance for a second. Time after time she raised her eyes to meet Declan's, wanting reassurance, wanting anything to tell her they'd done the right thing. *I'm fine*, his look said, and he gave her the merest nod.

'Thanks, team. Fantastic effort.' Declan inserted the last suture in Jodi's shin. He dressed the site with care and signalled for Emma to reverse the anaesthetic. 'How's our girl looking, Emma?'

'She's looking good,' Emma said.

'That's what I like to hear.' Above his mask, Declan's eyes crinkled with tired humour. 'OK, guys, would you mind finishing up here?' He stepped back from the operating table, working his shoulders briefly. 'I don't want to keep Moira waiting for news any longer than necessary.'

'I'm sure we don't mind at all.' Emma paused

and then added barely audibly, 'That was a fine piece of surgery, Declan.'

Declan's eyes met hers and held. 'You made it easy, Dr Armitage.' With that, he turned on his heel and left the theatre.

Declan answered the clamouring of his aching back with a long hot shower. The whole day had begun to take on a surreal quality. The adrenalin rush he'd felt at the beginning of the operation had disappeared, leaving him flat. He didn't dwell on it. Instead, he dressed quickly and went to meet Emma at the nurses' station.

At his approach, Emma looked up and smiled. She had a lot to smile about. Jodi was in Recovery and doing well. 'Apparently, there's some dinner for us in the canteen. Betty's made us her special Turkish lamb casserole,' she said.

He raised his brows in mock awe. 'We'd better have second helpings, then.'

'Did you get all your follow-up done?'

'I reassured Moira and left a few post-op instructions with the night sister. Jodi should be stable enough to make the transfer to the Royal late tomorrow. Her parents are flying back in the morning. They'll make their base in Brisbane for the next few days and see their daughter settled in.'

Emma nodded. She had a dozen questions for

him, about him, but none she could ask. Not yet. And maybe she wouldn't have to ask them at all. Maybe, without her prompting, Declan would simply tell her what she wanted to know. Had to know.

They ate hungrily.

'Not half bad,' Declan said, finishing his meal and placing his cutlery neatly together on his dinner plate.

'And so sweet of Betty to have made it especially for us.' Emma sent him a half-smile. 'Word's got round pretty quickly that big things happened here today.'

'Is that so?'

Emma stood up. 'Cup of tea?'

'Sounds good.' He turned away as his mobile phone rang.

Emma placed their cups of tea on a tray, added some rosemary shortbread she'd raided from the nurses' cookie jar and began making her way back to their table. It was late and they were the only ones left in the hospital canteen. Although he hadn't said it, Declan must be feeling the strain of the day, she thought. The charcoal shadows around his eyes were a dead giveaway.

Well, they'd be home soon. She'd hold him all night, smooth away the tensions, pleasure herself with the hardness of his body and the careless male beauty of his nakedness. They'd made love only this morning but it already felt like a year ago.

Her breath felt fluttery.

'Drink up and we'll make tracks.' Declan's brow furrowed. 'I'll drop you home and then take off. I need to wind down a bit and I want to make a call to Scotland. Have a chat to Angus Menzies at St Mary's about today. Debrief, I guess.'

Why couldn't he debrief with *her*? A look of disbelief scorched Emma's gaze. Hell, she'd been there with him at the cutting edge. It was only because of her compliance that he'd been able to go ahead and perform the surgery at all. She couldn't believe he wouldn't want them to spend the night together. 'You could do all that from Kingsholme.'

Of course he could. But he knew that would mean Emma would want him, *expect* him, to stay the night. To make love with her. How could he tell her he doubted if he was physically capable? The hours spent in surgery had left him with a burning pain in his lower back, his legs feeling as if he'd run a marathon. It was too soon to know if it would be an ongoing problem for him. But hell, what if it was? He gathered the strands of his tattered pride, raising an eyebrow at her. 'I've got a bit to sort out. You know how it is.'

No, she didn't know at all. Her confidence in their new-found commitment dropped to the floor. And stayed there like an unwanted garment that didn't fit. Lifting a hand, she brushed an imaginary crumb from her bottom lip. 'I'm ready when you are, then.'

They made their way in silence to his car. When they arrived at Kingsholme, Declan walked her to the door. 'I thought we could meet up at the hospital in the morning. See Jodi together. Around eightish? Is that all right with you?'

'Fine.' Emma shrugged. 'I hope you get your debrief.'

'Mmm.' He leant and placed a swift little kiss on her mouth and then stepped back. 'Thanks for today,' he said abruptly then walked away.

The house felt cold and unlived-in. Emma shivered. She went from room to room, switching on the lights. She could have a fire. But why bother? The empty feeling inside her was terrible.

What was going on with Declan? Physically, he appeared to have coped with the long stint in the OR. But he hadn't enlightened her about how he was feeling. Surely she deserved more than the cursory thanks he'd offered? Unless—Emma felt a river of alarm run down her spine. Was he intending to walk away now he had his career back? He'd said she had to trust him, but just now her trust was wearing very thin. Gossamer-thin and fragile.

The next morning, there was no sign of Declan when Emma arrived at the hospital. She decided to go and visit Jodi without him. He'd made the arrangements. It was up to him to keep them. Or let her know if he couldn't for some reason.

She found Jodi sitting up in bed, looking pale. Well, that was to be expected. The youngster had undergone major surgery. 'Hi, sweetie.' Emma pulled up a chair and sat down. 'How are you feeling?'

'I've been better.' Jodi pulled a sad little clown's face. 'I *so* cannot believe what happened.'

'They call them accidents, honey. All said and done, you were very fortunate.'

Jodi made a sound of disgust in her throat. 'The guys got off scot-free.'

'Except for getting the fright of their lives—and I think Mr McGinty will have a few hard words to say to them,' Emma predicted soberly.

Hell. Declan dragged a pair of jeans and a long-sleeved sweatshirt out of the pile of clean laundry and dressed hurriedly. How on earth could he have slept in? He hadn't heard the alarm. Well, what did he expect? He'd spent most of night wide awake before sleep had finally claimed him around 4:00 a.m.

And he hadn't solved anything. He still felt caught in a sea of confusion. He felt bad about how he'd handled things with Emma last night. Or not handled them. With hindsight, he knew he should have told her how physically exhausted he'd felt. She would have understood. But then that would have opened another can of worms—should he have operated at all?

Now he was facing an even worse scenario. By the way he felt this morning—would he ever be able to operate again? Grabbing his jacket, phone and car keys, he stepped out into the chilly morning.

He wasn't surprised to see Emma's little four-by-four in the parking lot when he arrived at the hospital. He shook his head. She was always so reliable, did things by the book. Except for yesterday. His mouth twisted grimly. He knew that backing him to do the surgery had been a huge call for her. Right outside her comfort zone.

Entering the hospital, he flung a greeting at the nurse on duty at the station and made his way along the corridor to Jodi's room. Taking a deep controlling breath, he knocked and entered.

'Morning.' Both women looked up. Emma held his gaze for a second, then looked pointedly away. He winced inwardly. She was cheesed off with him and he didn't blame her. He picked up Jodi's chart and studied it. 'How's our star patient this morning?'

Jodi managed a half smile. 'I'm still here. I guess that's a plus.'

'A pretty big plus from where I'm standing.' Declan raised his dark head. 'And I dare say Emma feels the same. How's the pain this morning, Jodi?'

'Still hurts a bit.'

A lot, Declan interpreted, going on the night report. 'I'll up your pain relief. That should help.'

'Nan says I have to go to Royal Brisbane. Is that really necessary?'

''Fraid so.' Declan replaced the patient chart and pocketed his pen. 'We don't have the facilities to nurse you here, Jodi. Besides, you're going to need some specialized rehab to get your legs back in working order.'

Emma squeezed Jodi's hand. 'You're young and fit, Jodi. You'll be back with us before you know it.'

'And what *about* my legs?' Jodi's voice wobbled. 'How badly hurt were they? Will I be able to ride again? Can I have the truth, please…?'

Emma glanced at Declan, then snatched her gaze away as if it hurt her eyes. 'They're probably questions for your surgeon,' she said and held Jodi's hand tightly.

'I won't keep the truth from you, Jodi.' Declan slipped seamlessly into a role he knew so well. Dealing with the anxieties of post-surgery patients. 'Your legs were pretty badly knocked about.' At Jodi's little gasp of dismay, he lifted a staying hand and went on, 'But I've done this kind of operation dozens of times. You're back together.' He smiled then. 'And almost as good as new.'

'Oh—' Jodi gave a little mew of relief.

'If you work hard with your physio,' Declan promised, 'your fitness will return quite quickly.'

'And my legs… Will…will they look…gross?'

'Of course they won't!' Emma looked appalled. 'I won't regale you with the clinical details of the operation, but Declan did an amazing job. You'll find there'll be hardly any scarring at all.'

Jodi sent them a watery smile. 'Thanks.' She leaned back on her pillows, her look braver than before. 'And what about my job at the surgery?'

'Well, I don't know about that.' Declan rubbed his jaw as if considering a weighty problem. 'What do you think, Emma?'

Emma did her best to join in the light-heartedness for Jodi's sake. 'Oh, I think we can muddle along until you can come back to us, sweetheart.' She got to her feet. 'Now, we'll leave you in peace.'

'Nan said she'd be in a bit later on.' Jodi blocked a yawn. 'Are you both coming in to see me off on the chopper?'

'Wouldn't want to be anywhere else, would we?' Emma placed a gentle hand on Jodi's shoulder. 'I'll check with the nurses' station about the ETA of the CareFlight chopper.' She fluttered a wave in Jodi's direction and made her way to the door. Declan followed closely behind.

Emma waited until they were outside the hospital before she asked, 'You do intend being here to see Jodi safely off, don't you, Declan?'

He shoved his hands into the back pockets of his jeans. 'I...need to talk to you about that. Could we go somewhere for a coffee?'

Emma sent him a speaking look. 'You mean you'll actually make time for me?'

He hunched his shoulders and scrubbed at a pebble with the toe of his shoe.

'Emma, this is very hard,' he said. And she could see in the strained expression in his face how much he meant it.

'It doesn't have to be, does it?' she countered, her throat tight. 'You could just talk to me.'

'I can't—not yet. A lot's happened over the last

twenty-four hours. I need to find my own way through this. Please understand.'

Was he saying he couldn't share his thoughts with her? Or was it something deeper? Her mouth drooped. Whatever it was, she knew she couldn't push him any further. She glanced at her watch. 'Rina Kennedy is reopening the garden centre today. I promised I'd go along. They've incorporated a food court in the refurbishment. We could get a coffee there.'

'Fine,' he agreed quickly. 'I'll follow you.'

The garden centre was already buzzing. Quashing her immediate problems, Emma looked around her. The townsfolk had come out in droves to support the Kennedys. And it was looking lovely. Very upmarket.

Declan touched her arm. 'This looks like the coffee shop through here. Shall we get a table?'

Emma nodded, the well of emotion rising in her throat threatening to choke her. When they were seated, she picked up the menu and made a pretence of studying it. 'Well, this is different,' she joked thinly. 'Fancy a wattle seed tea?'

Declan's mouth twisted in the parody of a smile. 'I'll stick to coffee, thanks. But don't let me stop you. What about some raisin toast to go with it?'

'I'll have a friand, I think.' She turned to catch the eye of the waitress and blinked. 'Oh, my goodness—there's Tracey! She must work here.' She was looking wonderful in her pristine white T-shirt and black pants covered by a dark green apron with the little shamrock embroidered on the front. Her hair was pulled neatly back and her smile was wide and welcoming as she approached their table.

They exchanged greetings and Tracey said, beaming, 'I've got a job here.'

'Congratulations,' Declan said warmly.

'From me as well,' Emma added. 'You're a star, Tracey.'

'I got the job off my own bat too,' Tracey said proudly. 'Mrs Kennedy is going to teach me the nursery side of things and I can do some college courses in Toowoomba and learn how to propagate plants and stuff.'

'That's brilliant.' Declan raised dark brows. 'I'm impressed.'

'Well, I've you to thank really, Dr O'Malley.' Tracey blushed. 'I mean you believed in me...'

Declan shook his head. 'You did all the hard work, Tracey.'

'Maybe...' She bit her lip. 'And Dr Armitage—you looked after my kids...' She stopped, embarrassed.

'It was a pleasure, Tracey.' Emma blinked a bit. 'They're wonderful kids. Are they here today?'

'Heck, no.' Tracey rolled her eyes. 'They're with Nev.'

'So, life is looking pretty good, then?' Declan asked.

Tracey nodded. 'And, best of all, I've been placed on the Defence Department's housing list. The kids and I should get our own place pretty soon. We'll be together again and Carolyn will get some peace at last. Anyway...' she huffed an embarrassed laugh and took out her order book '...what can I get you?'

There was an awkward silence after Tracey had gone.

'So, did you manage your debrief?' Emma's question had a sharp edge to it.

His look was guarded and cool. 'After a fashion.'

'Look, could we stop talking in riddles?' Emma threw caution to the winds and said what was uppermost on her mind. 'It hurt that you didn't want us to be together last night. What am I supposed to think now, Declan?'

'I hardly know what to think myself, Emma,' he said baldly. 'Yesterday changed everything.'

'You mean it's given you options you didn't have before, don't you?'

Declan's face was tightly drawn. 'I don't know yet. That's something I have to find out.'

The silence between them lengthened and became thicker.

'I need to ask a favour of you, Emma,' he said at last.

Her heart pounded uncomfortably. 'What do you need?'

'I need to be in Melbourne for a couple of days. I'll get a flight today from Brisbane and I should be back for surgery on Tuesday. If you could cover my patient list on Monday, I'd be grateful.'

She was hardly surprised at his request. It wasn't as though she hadn't conducted surgery countless times before on her own. It was obvious he was going to Melbourne to sort out what options were open to him. Maybe even get a new job operating now he knew he could. Well, she hoped he got what he wanted. He certainly didn't want *her.* She took a deep breath and pressed her palms down hard on the table. 'Go and do what you have to do, Declan. I'll manage.'

CHAPTER TWELVE

'MOIRA, streamline the patient lists as much as you can, please,' Emma said on Monday morning to the practice manager. 'I'm covering for Declan today.'

'Where *is* Declan?' Moira raised a questioning brow.

'Melbourne,' Emma said economically.

'He has family in Melbourne, doesn't he?'

'Yes.' Emma shrugged. And Declan was known there, had a network of professional contacts there. No doubt felt at home there. Enough to draw him back?

Her nerves tightened alarmingly. If he knew he could resume his chosen discipline, what on earth could entice him to stay in Bendemere?

The thought was painful. Almost impossible to bear. But Emma brought her fair head up determinedly. 'Don't worry about morning tea, Moira. I'll work straight through to lunch.'

Declan waited in the foyer of the lovely old building that contained within its hallowed architecture the professional rooms of the city's leading specialist doctors.

No one knew he was in Melbourne. No one apart from Emma and Matthew Levingston, one of Australia's top spinal consultants, who had agreed to see him first thing this morning as a professional favour. He hadn't wanted to tell his sisters he was in town. There would be too many questions—questions he didn't have answers to.

The lift arrived and Declan stepped inside. Even though he'd had only tea and toast for breakfast, it was sitting uneasily in his stomach. Breathing out a jagged breath, he pressed the button for the third floor.

Dr Levingston's receptionist, Jill Carter, was middle-aged and pleasant, her smile professionally in place as Declan approached the counter.

'Declan O'Malley.' His voice was clipped, strained. 'I have an appointment this morning.'

'Yes, Dr O'Malley. Dr Levingston is expecting you. Take a seat for a moment. He shouldn't be long.'

'Thanks.' Declan hesitated. 'Would you know if my notes arrived from Scotland? They were coming from St Mary's in Edinburgh.'

'Faxed through during the weekend. Doctor has them now.'

Declan nodded, relieved. That was the first

hurdle over, then. He crossed to where a row of comfortable chairs were arranged along the wall and lowered himself into one of the cushioned seats. He stretched out his legs and looked at his watch for the umpteenth time. It was barely eight o'clock.

It seemed only seconds later when a side door opened and the consultant poked his head out. 'Declan. Come through, mate.'

The two men shook hands warmly. 'Thanks for seeing me at such short notice, Matt,' Declan said.

'Happy to do it.' The consultant's mouth twisted into a wry grin. 'Have to look after our own, don't we? Now, could I organize coffee?'

Declan's stomach protested. 'No—no, thanks. I'm fine.'

'Right, let's put you through your paces, then.'

Matthew's examination was painstaking, his questions, and Declan imagined there were a thousand of them, probing. 'OK,' he said finally. 'That's it for now. Anything you want clarified?'

'The residual pain I experienced after I'd been in Theatre?'

'Pretty normal. It would have helped if you'd been able to ease yourself back into work rather than go for a seven-hour marathon straight away,' he suggested dryly.

'I was faced with an emergency,' Declan said. 'Not much choice there.'

'Probably not.' Matthew's mouth pursed thoughtfully. 'You can get dressed now, Declan. Come back out when you're ready and we'll have a chat. It's looking good, by the way,' he added before pulling back the screen and returning to his desk.

Declan felt one layer of trepidation roll off him. One step at a time, though. That was all it could be until he knew...

'You appear to have healed particularly well,' said Matthew. 'Your spine is in good order.' He amplified the statement with technical language because he rightly guessed Declan would want the clinical assessment. 'Now, all that said, I'd like you to have an MRI before I can give you definitive answers.'

Declan gave a resigned grin. 'I was afraid you'd stick me with one of those.'

'You betcha. But, with the new technology, they're less onerous than they used to be.' Matthew picked up his phone and spoke briefly to his receptionist. 'Do the best you can,' he ended. 'Thanks.' He clipped the phone back on its cradle. 'There's normally a bit of a wait on these. How soon do you need to be back at your practice?'

In an instant Declan was transported back to

Kingsholme, visualizing Emma beavering away through the morning's list, her fair head bent over the patients' notes. She probably hadn't had a moment to think of him. But he'd had the whole of the weekend to think of her. And she was filling his heart to overflowing. But his feelings were laced with vulnerability. Such vulnerability. He wasn't sure of her or her feelings for him. 'My partner is holding the fort but I'd like to get back as soon as possible.'

Matthew nodded, his hand reaching out as his phone pad lit discreetly. He leaned back in his chair, holding the receiver loosely and listened. 'OK, thanks, Jill. Excellent. We're in luck,' he said, replacing the handset. 'The imaging centre has a cancellation. How does ten-thirty sound?'

Although he wasn't particularly looking forward to the procedure, Declan nodded gratefully. 'Sounds good. Which centre do you use?'

'The new state-of-the-art set-up in St Kilda. Jill will give you the address. Then I'll need to see you again and discuss things.' Matthew pulled his diary open and studied it. 'I'm not in Theatre today so I could see you, let's see—around four this afternoon?' he suggested, sending a quizzical glance across his desk.

'I'll be here.' The two men stood and shook hands again.

'A word of advice, Declan,' Matthew said as he saw his patient out. 'Don't spend the day sweating about outcomes. I'll see you back here at four.'

Outside the building, Declan took a moment to get his bearings. He hardly remembered getting here this morning, so totally preoccupied as he'd been with the weight of his medical appointment. Now, he felt better, freer. The worst was over. His fitness hadn't lapsed and, whatever the outcome of the MRI, he knew now he could make a life for himself in medicine, even if it couldn't be permanently in the operating theatre. He'd enjoyed being a family practitioner more than he'd ever thought he would.

The feeling of optimism startled him, refreshed him. God, it felt good just be out in the world again, in a city he loved.

Suddenly he longed to share his news with someone who cared. He grimaced. Emma was out of the question. He had a lot of making up to do before he could expect her to listen to him. Both his sisters would be at work. Hailing a passing cab, he got in and gave the St Kilda address of the imaging centre. Then it came to him. There *was* someone he could talk to.

At the airport, Declan prowled past the ticketing booth yet again. He'd been waiting on standby for his flight to Brisbane. Several flights had been called but each time he'd missed out on a seat. Another flight was about to depart and he *had* to get on board if he was to have any chance of seeing Emma tonight.

He almost missed his name when it was called. Finally. Thank God. He looped his carry-on bag over his shoulder and strode swiftly down the covered walkway to the waiting aircraft.

Emma sat on the sofa in a kind of twilight daze. Earlier, she'd been for a run and on her return she'd showered and dressed in her track pants and fleecy top. She supposed she should go to bed but she knew she'd never sleep. She'd had one brief text message from Declan telling her he'd be back some time tonight. She wondered how late his flight had got in.

She should have swallowed her pride and texted back and insisted he stay the night in Brisbane. With the possibility of a fog always present, driving up that mountain road at night was fraught with risks.

When the knock sounded on the back door, she lifted her head sharply towards the sound, her heart swooping. Swallowing back a little cry of anguish, she half-ran, half-walked to the door. Reaching for the latch, she yanked it open.

Seeing him there, smiling, expectant, in one piece, when she'd envisaged all kinds of calamities, she felt suddenly overwhelmed by anger. 'What time do you call this, Declan? It's after midnight!'

The amber in her eyes glittered like fiery embers. She was beautiful and he suddenly realized he couldn't wait a moment longer to tell her how he felt about her. Feeling he was opening up his chest and showing her his heart, he said, 'I love you, Emma. I'm never letting you go.'

'Ooh—' Emma felt all the breath leave her body, a great jumble of emotions tumble around inside her. Was she dreaming? She stood frozen, love, hope and joy colliding in a great ball in her chest.

'Emma?' His eyes clouded. 'I'm freezing to death here. Did you hear what I said?'

She gave a frenzied little nod and found her voice. 'Come inside then, you crazy man.' She drew him inside to the warmth of the lounge room. And turned to him, eyes overbright. 'You must have been mad driving up the range at this time of night.'

'I must have been.' His eyes glinted and he reached for her and pulled her hard against him. 'Mad for the sight of you,' he said hoarsely. 'Do you love me too?'

Emma took a deep breath, feeling overwhelmed suddenly by recent events. 'Of course I love you.'

'Oh, thank God,' he whispered. 'Thank *you*,' he echoed, pressing kisses all over her face. 'I never want to be away from you again.'

They were words she'd longed to hear. But she wasn't letting him off the hook just yet. 'You owe me an explanation, Declan. I've been going slowly crazy wondering where your head was at for these past couple of days. Did I do something wrong— say something wrong?'

'No! It wasn't you—it was me. After Jodi's surgery, I was so preoccupied with my own problems, I wasn't thinking straight.'

'We *should* have debriefed,' she insisted. 'I needed it as much as you.'

'Yes, you did. I honestly didn't realize.' He frowned down into her face. 'I wasn't feeling all that great after Jodi's surgery,' he confessed, his voice a bit scratchy. 'But I didn't want to burden you. I'd pushed you to support me and I was afraid my career might be completely over—that you'd be forever lumbered with a practice partner—and a lover—who couldn't pull his weight…'

'Oh, my God—Declan!' Emma shook her head as if she couldn't believe his thought processes.

'I know, I know,' he admitted ruefully. 'It all sounds a bit pathetic and over-reactive now.'

'Shh.' She placed her fingers on his lips. 'It was a big deal for you. I should have understood that. I guess I was a bit selfish.'

'You're the least selfish person I know,' he countered.

Emma curled her fingers up around his neck. 'Are you terribly tired—or could we talk?'

The curve of her bottom through the soft stuff of her track pants felt good tucked into his palms and he shook his head. 'I'll never be too tired for you, Emma.'

They stoked up the fire and fell on to the sofa in a tight tangle of arms and legs, her cheek pressed against his chest so that she could hear the steady rhythm of his heart. 'So—' she paused and reached up to touch his face, stroking the dark shadows around his eyes with gentle fingers '—what did you do in Melbourne?'

His brain fizzed with technical information but he kept it simple, telling her about his medical appointments but leaving nothing out.

'And what did Dr Levingston say when you went back to see him?' She almost held her breath for his answer.

'That I'm fully recovered.' He looked suddenly

youthful, eager. 'I can operate again without fearing I'll fall over.'

'Oh, Declan!' Emma's pulse trebled before she could put the brakes on. 'I'm so happy for you,' she said, but thinking also what this new state of affairs could mean to them personally, to their practice, if he wanted to leave… 'It's going to change things here, isn't it?'

'Only if it's what we both want.' He looked down at her, his face unsmiling, deep in concentration. 'I had plenty of time to think while I was waiting for a flight home. I came up with a couple of possibilities.'

'OK…' Emma felt a hard-edged little lump that lodged somewhere in her chest. 'Tell me.'

'Well, we could leave things as they are,' he said slowly. 'I'm sure I could schedule enough orthopaedic work in Toowoomba to keep my hand in, as well as pulling my weight here in the practice.'

Emma looked doubtful. 'Would that be fulfilling enough for you, though?'

'Yes,' he said without hesitation. 'If that's what you want too. I've learned a lot here. Being a doctor in a rural practice carries clout, enables you to get things done for people. Good things. Necessary things. It's a great feeling.'

Oh, she was so glad he felt like that. 'That's what I think too.'

He smiled. 'Yes. I knew that.'

'And we could open up the OR here and do basic procedures, like Dad did,' Emma expanded. 'Rachel's staying, by the way. I talked to her yesterday.'

'That's good. She's needed here.'

Emma noticed he'd gone quiet. He looked tired, she thought. And a little strained. It made her love him more. Made her want to smooth out those lines around his eyes and mouth with her fingers, and with her lips... They'd get to that. Later. 'What was the other possibility you came up with, then?'

'Ah!' There was life in his face again. 'I thought we could lease out the practice for a year and go and live in Melbourne.'

'Melbourne?' This was right out of left field. Emma wriggled upright. 'What would we do there?'

'I could go back to the OR full-time, be part of a surgical team again.'

'I see.' A tiny frown came to rest between her brows. 'And what would I do?'

'You, my love, could get a place in an anaesthetist training programme, upgrade your skills so you could be my gas woman when we come back to Kingsholme.'

She chuckled. 'Your gas woman? I like the sound

of it, though. But would I get into a programme? I imagine places are at a premium.'

'I know a few faces,' he said modestly. 'And I imagine if you used your dad's name in the right places, doors would open.'

Emma digested all that. The idea appealed to her. Quite a lot, actually. 'I think I'd really, really like to do that,' she said quietly. 'But we'd need to get someone of calibre for Kingsholme.'

'We would. If we offered a year's tenure, we'd be sure to get quality applicants.'

'And we *will* come back to Kingsholme eventually, won't we?'

'Of course we will,' he promised. 'We'd want to raise our kids here, wouldn't we?'

'Oh, yes… I'd love to fill the house with our children.' He looked startled and she wrinkled her nose and compromised, 'With two or three, then.'

'That's manageable.' He sliced her a grin and then sobered. 'You've been bowed down under tremendous pressure for a long time now, Emma. A year away will be good for you to do something for yourself, be a student again.'

She rolled her eyes at him. 'I'll probably end up with some pedantic authoritarian boss who'll yell at me.'

'Yell back.' Declan ran the tip of his finger

down her straight little nose. 'You're a fully qualified doctor, not some poor intern struggling for approval.'

'Mmm.' She settled herself more comfortably in his arms. 'It's pretty exciting to think we could do something like this, isn't it, Declan?'

'I think so.' He paused and rested his chin on the top of her head. 'I had lunch with Roz while I was in Melbourne.'

Emma twisted to look at him. 'You had lunch with my mother! Why?'

'I was at a loose end. Felt the need for family but Erinn and Katie were at work. Then I thought of your mum and it just seemed to fit. If I couldn't have you with me, then I had the next best thing. Roz was brilliant. We got on like a house on fire. We talked about you a lot.'

'Did you tell her why you were in Melbourne?'

'Yes. She was sympathetic, practical. Talked me up. I also told her I was in love with you.'

'You did?' Emma laughed. 'What did she say?'

'Said she'd gathered how things were between us when she stayed here recently. She approves, by the way.'

Emma gave him a quick intense glance. He'd taken her breath away.

'And she gave me something for you as well,'

Declan said. 'A photo album she thought you'd like to have. It's in the car.'

'Oh, Lord,' Emma groaned. 'Not nude baby shots—please?'

His head went back in a laugh. 'One or two. But mostly they're of you and your parents from when you were tiny until your teens. Your parents had a happy marriage, Emma. You can't fake the kind of warmth I saw in those snapshots.'

'I'd come to that conclusion myself,' she said softly, drawing closer to him. 'But it was sweet of Mum to send the album.' And put her last remaining fears to rest. Emma wanted to say it but her heart was so full she couldn't find the words and anyway he didn't give her time.

'Will you marry me, Emma?'

The words were bliss to her ears. She hesitated and then said, 'Yes, Declan, I'll marry you. But not yet.'

His dark brows shot up in question.

'I want us to do some old-fashioned courting first.'

He reached out and brought her chin up gently, and his eyes when they looked into hers were lit with devilment. 'You want me to *court* you?'

'Yes, please.'

'Like with flowers and presents and...love notes?'

'All of those.'

'And dinners out?'

She looked dreamily at him. 'And dinners in.'

'I can do that.' He kissed her very sweetly, very tenderly. 'And when I've done everything to your satisfaction, you'll become my bride?'

'Yes, Declan…' Her voice broke on a whisper as she looked up at him and saw the soft sheen of love in his eyes. 'Then I'll become your bride.'

MEDICAL™

Large Print

Titles for the next six months…

February

WISHING FOR A MIRACLE	Alison Roberts
THE MARRY-ME WISH	Alison Roberts
PRINCE CHARMING OF HARLEY STREET	Anne Fraser
THE HEART DOCTOR AND THE BABY	Lynne Marshall
THE SECRET DOCTOR	Joanna Neil
THE DOCTOR'S DOUBLE TROUBLE	Lucy Clark

March

DATING THE MILLIONAIRE DOCTOR	Marion Lennox
ALESSANDRO AND THE CHEERY NANNY	Amy Andrews
VALENTINO'S PREGNANCY BOMBSHELL	Amy Andrews
A KNIGHT FOR NURSE HART	Laura Iding
A NURSE TO TAME THE PLAYBOY	Maggie Kingsley
VILLAGE MIDWIFE, BLUSHING BRIDE	Gill Sanderson

April

BACHELOR OF THE BABY WARD	Meredith Webber
FAIRYTALE ON THE CHILDREN'S WARD	Meredith Webber
PLAYBOY UNDER THE MISTLETOE	Joanna Neil
OFFICER, SURGEON…GENTLEMAN!	Janice Lynn
MIDWIFE IN THE FAMILY WAY	Fiona McArthur
THEIR MARRIAGE MIRACLE	Sue MacKay

MILLS & BOON®

MEDICAL™

Large Print

May

DR ZINETTI'S SNOWKISSED BRIDE	Sarah Morgan
THE CHRISTMAS BABY BUMP	Lynne Marshall
CHRISTMAS IN BLUEBELL COVE	Abigail Gordon
THE VILLAGE NURSE'S HAPPY-EVER-AFTER	Abigail Gordon
THE MOST MAGICAL GIFT OF ALL	Fiona Lowe
CHRISTMAS MIRACLE: A FAMILY	Dianne Drake

June

ST PIRAN'S: THE WEDDING OF THE YEAR	Caroline Anderson
ST PIRAN'S: RESCUING PREGNANT CINDERELLA	Carol Marinelli
A CHRISTMAS KNIGHT	Kate Hardy
THE NURSE WHO SAVED CHRISTMAS	Janice Lynn
THE MIDWIFE'S CHRISTMAS MIRACLE	Jennifer Taylor
THE DOCTOR'S SOCIETY SWEETHEART	Lucy Clark

July

SHEIKH, CHILDREN'S DOCTOR...HUSBAND	Meredith Webber
SIX-WEEK MARRIAGE MIRACLE	Jessica Matthews
RESCUED BY THE DREAMY DOC	Amy Andrews
NAVY OFFICER TO FAMILY MAN	Emily Forbes
ST PIRAN'S: ITALIAN SURGEON, FORBIDDEN BRIDE	Margaret McDonagh
THE BABY WHO STOLE THE DOCTOR'S HEART	Dianne Drake

MILLS & BOON®